Bear Wings

second edition

Second edition
First edition published 2024.
Second edition (revised) published 2026.

A CIP catalogue record for this book is available from the British Library.

Paperback ISBN 978-1-0685153-3-0
Hardcover ISBN 978-1-0685153-4-7
Kindle ISBN 978-1-0685153-5-4

River Linnsight
Bear Wings

PRAISE FOR BEAR WINGS

"One of the *most magical and heartwarming fantasies* I have read since *Philip Pullman's His Dark Materials*"

- Readers' Favorite

"From the moment I started reading this captivating children's novel, *I found it hard to put down until I finished reading it*. [...] This novel is a beautiful combination of reality, fantasy, and adventure. The plot reminds me of a cross between *Alice in Wonderland, Peter Pan, Harry Potter, and The Chronicles of Narnia*."

- Readers' Favorite

"*One of the most magical books I have ever read*. [...] Overall, this is a captivating start to the series, seamlessly blending adventure and introspection, and it is a *must-read for all fans of fantasy tales*."

- Readers' Favorite

"River Linnsight is a true wordsmith whose eloquent words create *a tale that will capture your heart and resonate with you long after the last page*."

- Readers' Favorite

"Beautifully written, insightful book that touches on deep themes. Utterly captivating, I can imagine a parent read this to a child or an adult losing themselves in the world created by the author."

- Amazon

To my beloved family,
whose unwavering support
is the foundation
of my existence.
R.L.

Author's note for the second edition

Bear Wings was born long before it was first published. When I began writing it with the intention of offering it to the world, my first literary love – poetry – flowed into the text, very much on purpose. I still hold that original version close.

Since then, two years spent writing and refining *Desert Wings*, the second instalment of *The Wings Trilogy*, have reshaped my understanding of clarity in prose. I've come to value the power of saying less, of allowing emotion and meaning to surface without concealment, and of guiding insight through precision rather than suggestion.

With that in mind, I returned to *Bear Wings*. The story remains unchanged; only its telling has evolved. This revised version aligns more closely with the voice and sensibility of the books that follow, should you choose to continue the journey. The connections to the wider *Wings* story are now clearer, the layers more visible, the language more refined.

I hope, dear reader, that you will enjoy the book, and that by its end, something within you will have quietly shifted.

“A ship in harbour is safe,
but that’s not what ships are built for.”
~J. A. Shedd

Trigger Warning: The content of this book includes themes of violence, murder, death, and mental health crises that may be disturbing or triggering for some readers. It also contains references to pirates' and other creatures' lore and language that may be considered harsh or offensive. Reader discretion is advised.

Note: Based on feedback from younger beta readers, we added a glossary to clarify less common terms. It provides concise, context-relevant definitions drawn from reputable sources, sometimes with alternative meanings to support learning, and to improve accessibility without diminishing the book's wider appeal.

Bear Wings

The Wings Book One

Contents

Prologue

In a room draped in time-worn shadows, a child lay still, his presence no more than a whisper of dust and forgotten sorrow. Motes of thought, stirred by the cadence of his breath, drifted and danced within a single beam of light. In the depths of his eyes, I glimpsed my own essence, long lost, stretching into the dim recesses of memory.

Beside him stood a figure in alabaster – a polar bear with fur faintly scented of flax. Its incomplete smile remained silent. Once a vessel of joy, now set aside, it could no longer still the storms of unspoken longing in the child's heart. Stitches loosened at its mouth, dark button eyes watching the shivering boy hugging his pillow. A trace of distant laughter lingered between the walls, already fading.

As light waned, a subtle yet profound change took hold. Amidst dusk's soft murmurs, the child found more than mere solace. An unforeseen connection that had taken seed long ago, not of this world, but born of whispered dreams, bloomed on the friendship's sapling.

Chapter I: The Awakening

«In shadows old, a child lay still,
Echoes of sorrows, dreams to fill.
Beside him stood, in silent white,
A bear, a friend, in darkest night.»

The boy couldn't sleep.

He lay curled at the edge of his bed, while the moon crept across the floor, touching his bookshelf, his desk, the pile of clean clothes his uncle kept bringing in that the boy never put away.

The room was full of things that used to matter: a LEGO castle on the shelf, half-built. A poster of planets on the wall, one corner peeling. A jar of collected rocks on the windowsill, labelled in his mother's handwriting.

He didn't look at any of it.

Three months. Ninety-one days, actually.

He had counted every one. Somehow that made him feel so old – like he'd been alive forever. The lilies were long gone, but the smell had soaked into the walls. Or maybe he just imagined it. He couldn't tell anymore what was real and what was the grief playing tricks.

Above him, on the shelf, sat Snowy – a polar bear. His friend. A toy older than memory could hold. Its coat was a patchwork of stitched seams and worn plush, white gone grey in places. A crooked smile because the stitches had come loose and the boy had never asked anyone to fix it. It looked sad.

The boy knew where the bear was. He'd slept with Snowy every night until he was eight. He could even reach it now with one hand. But the soft fur no longer comforted him; it only pricked at something raw.

Yet tonight, after everyone had gone home, the boy's eyes stayed open. They had been open for hours.

And in that hush, something small happened.

The bear tipped.

Not falling all at once, but as if tugged by an unseen thread – one slow, inevitable tilt – until it toppled from the shelf and landed against the boy's shoulder with a muffled thump.

It rested there, patient. Waiting.

The boy's hand moved before thought. He drew Snowy to his chest and held it like a secret. Pressed against his chest. Like it had always been. Eyes squeezed shut, breath trapped as if a wish might break if he let it out.

One tear slipped free. Then another. He didn't wipe them away. Didn't move at all. The tears fell to the starched linen with a sound as soft as breaking rain.

At the quiet toll, the bear's paw stirred.

It grazed the boy's cheek – soft as a butterfly's wing. Warmth seeped through worn plush, impossible and gentle. The paw found his shoulder and pressed, not quite a pat, not quite a hug: a gesture that felt like someone staying.

The boy opened his eyes.

Snowy's half-smile met his gaze – looking at him. Really looking. The button eyes weren't just buttons anymore. They were watching him.

Sad. Knowing.

"Hello, my friend," a voice said.

The boy froze.

Toys didn't talk.

Toys didn't move.

For countless nights Snowy had been there: when the boy had a toothache; when thunder made the world too loud;

when the dark pressed close. Snowy had always been a weight at his side, a small, faithful anchor. Snowy had never spoken. Not really. Only in his dreams.

But now it did.

"Snowy?" the child blubbered. "Is that really you? How... how did you..."

The bear chuckled. "You gave me life long, long ago. But I've been waiting for you to call me again." A pause, and the bear's tone warmed around the edges. "You named me, remember? You were four. You'd just read a book about polar bears and you pointed at me and shouted 'Snowy!' so loud your mother laughed."

The boy's chest tightened.

"She laughed a lot back then," Snowy added, quieter.

"Don't," the boy said.

Snowy's ears tilted. "Don't what?"

"Talk about her." The boy's hands curled into fists. "Because it hurts, okay? Because everyone talks like she's still here but she's *not* here. She's gone. And talking about her doesn't bring her back."

Snowy went still for a moment.

"No," the bear said at last, gentle but firm. "Talking doesn't bring her back." It shifted closer. "But not talking about her doesn't make her gone any less. It just makes her forgotten."

"I won't forget her," the boy whispered.

Snowy's head tipped to the side. "Won't you?" It watched him a beat. "When was the last time you thought about her laugh? Not that she's gone – that's all you think about. But the way her laugh broke when she tried not to laugh and failed?"

The boy opened his mouth. Closed it. He couldn't remember.

"That's what I thought," Snowy said, not unkindly. "Come

on, then." The bear's voice lifted, trying for brightness without lying. "Shall we go on an adventure?"

"I don't want an adventure."

"I know," Snowy said. "But you need one."

The bear stood on the bed and set its paws on its hips like a commander surveying a battlefield.

"And honestly?" it added. "So do I. Do you know how boring it is sitting on a shelf? I've memorised every crack in your ceiling. I've watched seventeen spiders build webs in the corner. I've counted specks of dust until I thought I'd go mad."

Despite everything, the boy felt his mouth twitch. Almost a smile. "You can't go mad. You're a toy."

"Can't I?" Snowy hopped down from the bed with more grace than a stuffed animal should possess. "What do you know about what toys can and cannot do? You stopped playing with me years ago."

The guilt hit like a punch. "I didn't mean—"

"I know you didn't," Snowy said quickly. The bear's voice softened, old warmth returning. "You got older. That's what happens. Children grow, and they put things away, and the world tells them that's how it should be."

Snowy looked up at him. The moonlight turned its button eyes into small, dark stars.

"But now you need me again," it said. "Will you let me?"

The boy stared at his bear, at the worn fur, the loose stitching of the smile, the paw that was slightly discoloured from the time he'd spilled juice on it when he was six and cried because he thought he'd ruined his favourite toy forever.

"Where would we go?" he asked quietly.

"Somewhere better than here," Snowy said. "Somewhere with more colours. More sounds." It hesitated, as if searching for a word that wasn't a lie. "More life. And fewer memories that bite."

"Can we really just... leave?"

"For a while. Yes." Snowy reached up and took his hand. The paw was soft, too soft, and warm. "But we must go soon. The door doesn't stay open long."

"What door?"

Snowy's crooked smile shifted. It became real. The bear pointed towards the corner of the room where the boy's winter coats hung.

The boy looked.

At first, he saw only shadows. The usual darkness pooling like spilled ink where moonlight couldn't reach. But then...

Light.

Thin lines of it, silver-white, drawing, burning brighter. A doorframe. Like someone was tracing it with a sparkler. But then the space inside the frame began to shimmer. Blue, like the morning sky. Like music he couldn't quite hear.

The boy's breath caught. "That's not... that can't be..."

"It is," Snowy said softly.

His fingers tightened on the frame when he reached it, as if it might vanish under touch.

He felt too old for this. He used to climb trees. Used to laugh so hard milk came out of his nose. Used to build elaborate traps with string and cardboard and absolute faith that the world was a place made for play.

That was before.

Before the lilies. Before everyone started speaking to him like he might shatter.

"Why are you scared?" Snowy asked, and for the first time the bear sounded nervous – truly nervous, as if even it didn't trust miracles. "If you don't want to, we can stay."

“Here?” The boy’s voice came out harder than he meant.

“There’s always a choice, cub,” Snowy said softly.

“Don’t call me that,” the boy whispered, and his heart fluttered like a trapped bird, bruising its wings against hope.

He stepped forward.

Crossed the threshold.

Behind him, the starlit door closed with a sound like a sigh.

And the boy didn’t look back.

Chapter II: The Surprise

«In moon's soft glow, where dreams take flight,
Toys whisper secrets to the quiet night.
Polar bear wakes, with memories in tow,
Adventure calls, come on, let's go.»

The boy stepped through the doorway onto clouds that shouldn't have held his weight but did. White and solid, like standing on frozen ocean foam. The sky above was blue – impossibly blue – cradling clouds like a mother's hands. Below, real ocean stretched to the horizon, and to the right, a beach of pure gold. Far away, almost out of sight, a few grey clouds tainted the horizon.

"Oh!" Snowy, now a full-sized polar bear, bounced. Actually *bounced.* "Oh, I'd forgotten! Look at it all!"

And it ran – lumbered, really – towards the edge of the cloud, skidding to a stop just before toppling over. Its paws scrambled, sending wisps of cloud drifting down like snow.

"You're acting weird," the boy couldn't help it. He laughed.

"Am I?" Snowy turned, and something in those eyes looked almost... young. Embarrassed. "I suppose I am. It's been so long since I was anywhere but your shelf." The bear's voice dropped. "Grief makes us forget things. Even the things we love." The bear shook itself, snow-white fur rippling. "But we're here now! And I intend to enjoy it. Come on!"

Before the boy could protest, Snowy grabbed his hand and jumped.

They *fell.*

The boy's stomach lurched into his throat. Wind screamed past his ears. He tried to scream but couldn't find breath. The ocean rushed up. Too fast.

Snowy's other paw traced something in the air, and suddenly they weren't falling; they were gliding, spiralling down in lazy circles while the boy's heart tried to escape through his ribs.

"YOU COULD HAVE WARNED ME!"

"Where's the fun in that?" Snowy was grinning.

They landed on the beach in a spray of golden sand.

The boy collapsed. His hands sank into warmth. His legs wouldn't stop shaking. "I hate you."

"No, you don't." Snowy was already splashing in the shallows, pawing at waves like a cub. "Come on! The water's perfect!"

"I think I'm going to throw up."

"Perfectly natural! First time flying always does that. Your mother—" Snowy stopped.

The boy looked up sharply. "What about my mother?"

"Nothing." But all that playful energy had drained away.

"No." The boy stood, anger giving him strength. "You said—"

"I said nothing."

"You're *lying*."

Snowy turned to face him, and suddenly it looked old again. Ancient. Tired. "Your mother flew too, once. When she was young. In dreams. She told you about it, when you were very small. You don't remember."

The boy felt like he'd been punched. "She never—"

"She did. You just forgot." The bear's voice was unbearably gentle. "Come. The water's warm."

At first, the boy stayed close to shore. Let waves crash over his knees, washing away the ache. The water was warmer than it should be. Saltier. It stung the scrapes on his elbows – had he fallen yesterday? Last week? Time felt wrong here.

"Stay within the rocks," Snowy called from the beach, half-buried in sand. "That's as far as I can reach if something goes wrong."

"Nothing's going to go wrong."

The water felt good. Clean. The opposite of his room with its stale air and closed curtains.

Hours passed. Or maybe it felt like hours. The sun refused to move. The boy swam – floated – let the sea take the weight of him. For the first time in months, his chest loosened. For the first time, breath came without a fight.

When at last his arms turned heavy from the shallows and the waves, he staggered out and dropped onto the sand beside Snowy.

The bear had built something: not a castle so much as a fort – low walls, shell-bright crenelations, stubby towers.

"When did you make this?"

"While you were swimming." Snowy patted down a corner with solemn care. "Seemed wise."

"Wise?"

"We may require fortifications." Snowy nodded to the horizon. "You never know what's out here."

The boy huffed a laugh. It startled him – the sound of it, the way it broke loose. Like a muscle remembering itself.

"What?" Snowy asked.

"You," he said, still smiling. "You're a polar bear building a sand fort."

Snowy drew itself taller. "I am a magical bear," it said, grave as law, "constructing a tactical fortification."

The boy laughed again. Properly this time. Strange and bright in his throat.

Snowy's smile softened. Then, gently, it faded.

"It's good to hear you laugh," Snowy said. "Little cub."

"I told you not to call me that."

"And I told you I'm a bear. We call young ones cubs."

Snowy went quiet.

"Your mother called you that once too."

The boy stilled. The warmth drained from his hands.

"She did?"

"Mmm. *'My little cub',*" Snowy said, and the words came out like a remembered lullaby. "When she tucked you in. You were three. I was there."

He didn't remember. The absence of it ached like hunger.

"Tell me," he said.

Snowy tilted its head. "What do you want to know?"

"Anything." The boy swallowed. "Everything." His voice broke on the edge of it. "No one talks about her anymore. They're afraid it will hurt. But it already hurts, Snowy. It hurts all the time." He stared at the line where the sea kept rewriting the shore. "So tell me. Please."

Snowy shuffled closer and leaned its soft weight against the boy's side. Together they watched the waves arrive and forget, taking back the ground beneath their feet.

"She sang," Snowy said at last. "Terribly."

The boy's mouth twitched through grief.

"She couldn't hold a tune to save her life. But she sang anyway – mostly when she cooked. It drove your father mad." Snowy's mouth curved. "Mad in the way people get when they're trying not to smile."

"What would he do?"

"Pretend to cover his ears." Snowy pressed its paws to the sides of its head in demonstration. "And she'd sing louder just to make him suffer."

Tears slid down the boy's cheeks. He didn't wipe them.

The salt belonged there.

"And she tried to garden," Snowy went on, voice low, as if speaking in a room where the dead might be listening. "She killed every plant she loved."

The boy made a small sound – half laugh, half sob.

"But she kept trying," Snowy said. "She said she liked the optimism of it. The faith that something might grow."

"Did anything?"

Snowy paused, as if searching through drawers of memory. "Once. A tomato plant." A soft chuckle. "One tomato. She took more pictures of it than of any birthday."

"Was it... good?"

"It was dreadful," Snowy said, delighted despite itself. "She made your father eat it anyway."

The boy was crying harder now, but the grief had shifted. It still hurt – only now it also held her shape.

"She loved you," Snowy said, and the sea quieted around the words. "So much it frightened her. Sometimes she would sit by your bed after you'd fallen asleep and watch you breathe, like she was trying to learn the rhythm by heart."

"I miss her," the boy whispered.

"I know," Snowy said, and wrapped its arms around him. "I know."

They stayed like that – bear and boy – while the sun finally remembered to move across the impossible sky.

When Snowy stirred again, it did so reluctantly, like pulling free of a warm dream.

"We should go," it said.

"Where?"

Snowy looked out at the bright emptiness. "I don't know yet."

The boy drew back. "You don't know?"

"I'm... improvising," Snowy admitted. "This is my first time through the door in a long time."

"But you're supposed to be the guide," the boy said, a flare of panic under the words. "The wise one."

Snowy blinked. "I'm a stuffed bear who's spent years on a shelf. I'm very wise."

The boy stared. Then – against his will – a laugh escaped him. Smaller this time, but real.

Snowy stood and shook sand from its fur with dignity it had not earned. "Here's what I do know: we keep moving. We find someone who knows more than we do. The way ahead is never clear." It offered a paw. "That's what makes it a road worth walking."

"That's not a plan," the boy said.

Snowy's paw stayed out. "Have you got a better one? Courage isn't the quenching of fear – it's the acceptance of it."

The boy thought. Found only silence. He took the paw.

They went towards a stand of scrub and low trees that shimmered at the edge of the beach like a mirage trying to become true.

"I smell something," Snowy said.

"What?"

"Old," Snowy murmured. "Familiar. Like stories that have slept too long."

"Do bears dream?"

"Toy bears," Snowy said, voice strange and faraway, "dream the dreams children put into them." It glanced at him. "And sometimes those dreams don't stay dreams."

They found nothing beneath the treeline – only more sand, more light, more silence.

But it didn't stop them. They ran anyway, racing across the bright blankness like explorers in a world that hadn't learnt its own edges, laughing as if laughter could map what sight could not.

When exhaustion finally caught them, it caught them gently. They fell onto the murmuring shore. The sun stitched warmth through hair and fur. The waves breathed their slow forgetting.

The boy woke first.

Snowy slept beside him, still as a charm. Its chest rose and fell, steady. Safe.

The sea glittered beyond the rocks – blue, impossibly blue – an invitation with teeth hidden beneath it.

Something lit behind the boy's ribs. Not grief. Not fear.

But a wish.

Adventure.

That wild bright pull he could never quite refuse.

I'll be back before Snowy wakes, he told himself.

He stood and ran – heart quick, breath spent, feet kicking up the sand.

Behind him, Snowy's voice tore up from sleep, broken with sudden fear, calling his name.

But the boy didn't hear.

He swam farther out, the joy taking him, pulling him towards the wide shimmering blue.

He surfaced near the rocks. Climbed them, slick with salt. Stood at the edge.

Below, the water darkened – blue bleeding into deeper blue, then into something that wasn't blue at all.

He stared into it.

And the sea stared back. As if it could hear his wish coming true.

Just a little farther.

The thought came like a whisper. Like permission.

Just to see...

He dove. Close at first, swimming parallel to the rocks. But the water pulled – gentle, insistent. And he let it pull him under for just a moment. Underwater, everything was blue and quiet. No one asking if he was okay. No one wanting to talk about it.

He surfaced, gasping.

The shore was gone.

No.

The boy spun, treading water. Searched for the gold beach, for Snowy, for the rocks.

Only grey. Grey water under grey sky. The whitecaps were tall now. Threatening.

"Help!" His voice cracked. "Snowy! SNOWY!"

The ocean swallowed his scream.

His arms burned. His legs felt like lead. The current pulled, pulled, pulled. He felt minuscule and adrift. His heart pounded as he fought the waves, each stroke a desperate battle.

Then: a sound. Deep. Rhythmic. Like breathing.

His head whipped around.

A ship.

Massive. Larger than a whale. The boy gasped, his alarm nearly causing him to drown, while the shadow of this monstrosity of wood loomed closer. Dark wood, slick with seaweed and barnacles. It heaved itself from the deep – rising not like a ship, but like something the sea had laboured over and finally birthed into the world.

Shouting above. The creak of ropes.

Something splashed beside him.

A net.

It tangled around his arms before he could swim away.

Rough fibres bit his skin as it pulled him up, up, water streaming from his clothes, the ocean falling away beneath his kicking feet.

"Got somethin'!"

"'Bout time!"

The boy hit the deck hard. Wood slammed into his cheek. He tasted blood and salt. He smelt tar and fish and something else – something wild and wrong.

"Well, well." The voice was low. Amused. "What've we got here?"

The boy looked up.

The pirate had a tiger's head.

Not a mask. Not a costume. An *actual* tiger's head – whiskers, fangs, amber eyes that gleamed with hunger. The body was human. Scarred. Muscular. Leather vest. But the head was pure predator.

The boy couldn't breathe.

"Bit scrawny, innit?" A cheetah-headed pirate prodded his leg with one boot.

"Could fatten him up." A crooked monkey grinned. "Couple weeks in the hold, feed him scraps—"

"Waste of time." The tiger pirate drew a dagger, testing its edge against one claw. "Just gut him now. Use him for bait."

"Now, now, me hearties." A lion pirate – clearly the captain – crouched beside him. His breath smelt like meat. "Let's not be hasty. This one's got a certain... flavour to him. Can't you smell it?"

A clawed hand gripped the boy's chin, tilted his head back. The boy tried to jerk away but the net held fast.

"Magic-touched," the captain purred. "Got the stink all over him." The captain's dark eyes narrowed to slits. "Question is... what's he worth?"

"N-nothing. I'm nobody. Please—"

"Well then." The captain stood. "Off to the galley with you, lad!" the captain barked. "If you're not good for anything else, you'll serve as supper."

"Captain!" the tiger protested. "I say we—"

"And I say he goes to the galley." The captain's voice dropped to a growl. "Unless you'd like to join him?"

The tiger backed down.

Two pirates hauled the boy up and dragged him across the deck. He caught glimpses: a monkey in the rigging, a

crocodile coiling ropes, a hyena sharpening something he couldn't see. None of them looked human. Not in the ways that mattered.

They threw him down a narrow staircase.

He landed hard in a hot, cramped space. It smelt like burnt onions and old meat.

"Oy! Careful with him!"

The boy looked up through tears. A zebra stood over a cutting board, chef's knife in hand. Unlike the others, this one's fur was crisp and clean. Dark eyes met the boy's with something that looked almost like kindness.

"Out." The zebra's voice was flat. "I'll handle it from here."

"Cook us up a feast from this scrawny dog, ye scallywag!" the monkey sneered. "Captain's orders. And don't take too long."

"Captain can wait." The zebra's voice dripped contempt. "Now get out of my kitchen before I season *you* instead."

The pirates left, grumbling.

"Blimey, I wish ye never made me one of yer own, ye scurvy dogs," the chef muttered under his breath. He waited until their footsteps faded, then crossed to the boy. Up close, the boy could see the exhaustion carved into his face. The way his hands trembled as he cut through the net.

"Easy now," he murmured. "Let's get ye free."

The ropes fell away. The boy scrambled backwards until his back hit a barrel.

"Don't ye worry none, young'un," the zebra said softly. "I'd never be hurtin' a soul." He set the knife down, palms raised. "I ain't like these heartless sea wolves."

In the dimly lit kitchen, the chef knelt.

"Name's Kofi. Though I don't much answer t' it these days. Crew call me 'Stripey' or 'Scallywag'... or worse."

"They're going to eat me," the boy whispered.

"Maybe." Kofi didn't lie. The boy noticed that. "Or maybe not. Depends on the captain's mood. Depends on whether ye're clever." The zebra turned back to the stove, where something bubbled in a large pot. "Ye hungry?"

The boy's stomach answered.

"Thought so." Kofi stood and ladled stew into a wooden bowl. Handed it over. "Eat up. Can't be thinkin' straight on an empty belly."

The bowl was warm. Real. The first real thing since he landed on this ship. He drank it down. Burned his tongue. Didn't care.

"What..." His voice cracked. "Who *are* you?" he asked when he could speak again.

Kofi laughed, bitter as brine. "Wrong question, lad. Right question is: what was I?" The zebra pirate touched his striped muzzle. "Answer? Human. Same as ye."

The boy stared.

"Curse. That's what it be. Cross a sea-witch, this is what ye get. Whole crew was human once. Captain too – Thanas, merchant by trade. Good man, they say."

His eyes dimmed like lanterns in fog.

"Witch offered power. Speed. Strength beyond reckonin'. They took it. Didn't see the cost 'till it swallowed them whole."

"The heads," the boy said quietly.

"The heads. The hunger. The sea callin' us back, ne'er lettin' us rest on land." Kofi stirred the pot. "Been eight years for me. Dropped a piece o' her silver overboard when I was a deckhand on another ship. She dragged me under, made me one o' them. Said I'd serve till I'd suffered enough t' know what loss truly meant."

"That's horrible."

"That's magic, lad. Always comes with a price." Kofi looked at him sharply. "Speakin' o' which – ye've got the stink o' it on ye. Where'd ye come from? How'd ye end up in these waters?"

The boy hesitated. Could he trust this creature? This cursed pirate, in a galley that smelt like death?

But what choice did he have?

"I came through a door," the boy said slowly. "Made of stars. With my polar bear – my toy. We were on a beach and I... I swam too far."

"To get away," Kofi said gently. It wasn't a question.

The boy nodded, throat tight.

"Aye, I've heard that story." The zebra leaned close, voice dropping to a whisper. "Old tales. Toys wakin' when children need them. Doors made o' wishes. Strange things." Kofi stopped, shook his head. "Point is – if yer bear's what I think, it'll come. Question is whether it'll come in time... and whether ye'll still be ye when it does."

"What does that mean?"

"Means the captain ain't just hungry for meat. Magic-touched folk? We can taste it. Consume it. Take it into ourselves." Kofi's voice was heavy. "If they eat ye, they'll swallow yer memories, yer dreams – whatever magic dragged ye here – it becomes theirs."

The boy felt cold despite the galley's heat. "Then what do I do?"

"Ye stay alive. Stay sharp. And you give me a reason t' help ye that the captain'll believe." Kofi slid a knife towards the boy. "So... can ye cook?"

The boy stared at the knife. At the zebra's tired eyes.

"My mum taught me," he said quietly. "A little. Before—"

"Before," the pirate nodded. "Then start choppin'. And while ye do, tell me everythin' 'bout this bear o' yours. If I'm riskin' my hide helpin' ye escape, I need t' know it's worth the trouble."

"Why?" The boy picked up the knife. "Why help me at all?"

Kofi smile flickered, half-formed. "In a world full o' monsters and curses and ships that eat boys, we all be needin' a wee drop o' kindness, lad. Don't ye think?"

They cooked.

The boy's hands shook at first. But the rhythm steadied him. Chopping the onions. Dicing the carrots. Peeling the purple yam – from the Southern Isles, Kofi said.

His mother had taught him to cook eggs once, when he was six. Had stood behind him, her hands over his, guiding the spatula. He'd burned them. They'd laughed.

The memory hurt. But less than it had before.

He told Kofi about his room. About the silence. About his polar bear, sitting on the shelf, the only thing that still felt real. And about how Snowy became a real polar bear in this world.

"Magic always costs something, lad," Kofi muttered as he stirred the pot. "But sometimes the price be worth payin'. Sometimes ye need the impossible just t' survive the unbearable."

Above them, something changed.

The ship's rhythm shifted. The creaking grew louder. More urgent.

Footsteps thundered.

Shouting.

The ship *lurched.*

The boy gripped the counter. "What's happening?"

Kofi moved to the porthole. Peered out. His striped face went pale. "Storm's rollin' in fast." His voice was tight. "Strange one, too. Look at the turn o' them clouds."

The boy pressed beside him at the small window. The sky was purple, flashing in the mottled colours of old bruises. Lightning crackled, but it moved *wrong*. Too slow. Like something alive.

The ship lurched again. Harder. Something crashed below deck. The shouting turned to shrieking.

The galley door slammed open. The captain stood there – soaked, blood on his claws. Behind him: chaos. Pirates running. Ropes snapping. Wind *screaming*.

"You!" The captain pointed at the boy. "This is your doing!"

"What? No, I didn't—"

"The storm follows the magic! *Always* does!" The captain took a step forward, eyes glinting. "You brought it here. To *my* ship!"

"Captain, wait—" Kofi moved between them.

"Out of my way, Stripey, or I'll gut you both."

But before the captain could attack, something *enormous* slammed into them.

Wood screamed.

"LEVIATHAN!" someone bellowed from above.

"This ain't over, lad," the captain snarled. His tail flicked once, twice, before he wheeled about and vanished up towards the helm.

The ship was breaking apart. The boy hit the floor. Slid. Barrels toppled, spilling grain and salt and dried meat. Kofi caught him. Held him steady. His zebra ears pinned back, voice low and urgent.

"We need t' move, lad. Now. While the crew's all distracted."

"Where?!"

"Longboat. Port side." Kofi grabbed his arm. "Do ye trust me?"

The boy looked into Kofi's eyes. Saw fear. But also determination. Kindness.

He thought of the pirates with their flashing weapons. Their loud threats.

And Kofi. Quiet. Cursed. Kind.

"Yes," the boy said.

"Then stay close. We'll slip through these sea-dogs an' vanish 'fore they know we're gone. Savvy?"

They climbed the stairs and burst onto the deck into hell.

Rain pelted down in sheets. The leviathan – a whale as wide as the ship, covered in wood-scales that glowed with that same sickly light as the storm, smashed through the ship's starboard with its tail. Wood exploded. The deck tilted violently.

Pirates scrambled, hacking at the creature with harpoons, but the weapons barely scratched its scales.

"The longboat!" Kofi shouted over the storm. "There!"

They ran. Slipped on wet wood. Another smash to the deck. It moaned.

The longboat dangled from ropes over churning sea.

"Can ye climb?"

"I think so!"

"Then go! I'll cut ye loose!"

The boy grabbed the rope. His hands were slick with rain. He started to climb over the railing—

"TRAITOR!"

The tiger. Charging. Claws extended.

"NO!" The boy screamed.

Kofi spun, blocked the tiger's attack with his forearm. The boy heard bone *crack*. The zebra cried out but didn't fall. Shoved the pirate backwards.

"Go!" Kofi screamed. "NOW!"

"But—"

"I said GO!"

Kofi's knife flashed. One rope snapped. The longboat swung wildly. The zebra reached for the second rope—

The tiger tackled him.

They went down together. Rolling. Fighting. The tiger's claws found Kofi's throat—

The boy couldn't watch. Couldn't—

The second rope snapped.

And the boy fell.

Hit the water hard. Went under. Salt and darkness and the muffled roar of the leviathan above—

When he surfaced, gasping, the ship was already distant. Burning now. Fighting with the leviathan, with all sails stretched taut. Pirates falling overboard. Swimming. Drowning.

He couldn't see Kofi.

The longboat bobbed beside him, still intact. The boy pulled himself in. Collapsed. He was shaking so hard his teeth rattled.

Around him, the storm was dying. The clouds were breaking apart. The leviathan released the ship – what was left of it – and sank back into the depths.

The ocean went still.

The boy lay on the bottom of the longboat and wept.

He didn't remember grabbing the oars. Didn't remember rowing. But when dawn came – soft and pink and wrong – he was far from the wreckage. His hands were bleeding. His arms screamed. But he'd rowed all night. Away. Always away.

He let the oars drop. Stared at his hands.

On his right wrist was a mark. Rope burn, thick and red, where he'd gripped the line to the longboat. Where Kofi had cut him free.

Where Kofi had *saved* him.

The boy touched the mark. It stung.

In a world full of monsters, someone's got to choose kindness.

Kofi had chosen. Even knowing the cost. Even cursed. Even surrounded by darkness.

He'd chosen light.

The boy touched the mark. It stung.

Sometimes the kindest souls lived in the deepest dark.

His eyes were heavy. So heavy. As dawn coloured the sky, exhaustion overtook him, and his thoughts of fear and relief faded into silence. He succumbed to a trembling sleep, his right hand, marked, still gripping the oar.

The boat drifted until it nudged the sandy shallows of an unknown shore.

Chapter III: The Island

«In a realm where ocean meets sky in greet,
A lad's tale twines around the pirates' feet.
With zebra's guile beneath the night's veil,
Away young'un sails, from their sight hails.»

The boy woke to silence.

He woke abruptly, limbs jerking as if still caught in a net. His mouth tasted of salt, throat raw from the scream. The air smelt green. Alive.

No rocking. No waves. Just silence and the soft pressure of heat overhead.

He sat up slowly. Pain answered everywhere. His shoulders burned from the oars. His palms were scoured and blistered. His right wrist throbbed where the rope had skinned it open. A mark raised, angry red.

Kofi had cut him free.

Kofi had...

He shoved the thought down before it could finish. Down into the same dark place as the funeral. The empty rooms. The silence at dinner. Things too far away, and too close to breathe around.

The longboat had beached itself on dark-green sand.

Not golden, like the shore where he'd landed with Snowy.

This sand was almost black, packed and cool under his fingertips despite the sun. Spiky shells shimmered like scattered jewels, half-buried in the grit beneath a dense canopy that leaned towards the water, as if the jungle itself were thirsty.

Behind him – the ocean. Not quiet. Not peaceful. Alive in

a way that didn't care about him.

Around the shore, the forest smelt strange. Dark and bitter. Full of noises he didn't recognise. Chittering and clicks. Low hoots. The wet rustle of something moving through undergrowth.

He turned, scanning – too fast, like he expected claws and fangs from every shadow.

Not the golden beach.

Snowy nowhere in sight.

The boy was alone.

He stood, testing his legs. They held. Barely. They felt wrong, as if they belonged to someone else. How long had he been rowing? All night, maybe into morning. Time had blurred after the ship sank. After Kofi...

Don't.

He looked at the rope burn again. Pressed it with his thumb. The sting made him hiss through his teeth.

In a world full of monsters...

He shook his head, hard, like he could dislodge the image. Kofi had chosen. Had saved him. Had died for him, probably. The tiger's claws. The burning deck. The boy in the longboat drifting away, unable to see, unable to help, unable to even be sure.

"Stop," he said out loud. His voice sounded thin, small, swallowed quickly by leaves.

He needed to find Snowy. That was the only thought that mattered. Find the bear. Figure out how to escape.

He walked the shoreline, scanning the dark sand. Shells and stones flashed in broken sunlight – white, red, blue. *Broken, like me*, he thought, and didn't know why it made his throat tighten.

He crouched and picked a few up. Smooth ones, tide-polished. Sharp ones that bit his skin. He didn't stop himself. His hands wanted something to do.

He braided strands of algae into cord. Wrapped shells and stones into it, one by one, making a bracelet. Then another. A necklace.

The rhythm steadied him. *Over-under. Pull tight. Breathe. Over-under.*

The world narrowed to his fingers and the simple proof that his hands could still make something instead of just losing everything.

When he finished, he pulled the boat higher onto the sand, leaving it to bask under the sun. If he had to run, to flee again,

he wanted it ready.

Then he looked up at the trees.

No sense going back to the ocean. Not yet. Left or right, the beach curved into the same dark green wall. But ahead...

Smoke.

Thick and grey, rising beyond the canopy. Too straight to be mist. Too steady to be chance.

Fire meant people. People meant danger: strange rules, wills he couldn't read. Uncertainty.

His mind flashed – pirates with animal heads. The captain's claws lifting his chin. Hunger.

And Kofi.

Trust, he thought. *Trust is delicate. Trust is dangerous. Sometimes it's all I have.*

He stepped into the jungle. The jungle closed around him. Light turned green, filtered through layers of leaves. Humidity wrapped his skin. The air smelt of rot and sweet sap and something metallic, like rain trapped in stone.

He walked carefully. Watched where he stepped. As if the earth could break and swallow him whole.

The smoke thickened. And thickened. Yet it never got close.

He pushed through a curtain of vines and suddenly the trees fell away, and he saw where the smoke was coming from.

Not a fire.

A mountain. A huge, dark cone rising beyond the canopy, its top ragged like a broken tooth. Old – old enough to withstand storms. A thick, steady plume fumed from a seam near the peak. The earth beneath his feet gave a faint, distant tremble, so slight he might have imagined it.

A volcano.

He laughed once, surprised.

Maybe, if he could climb high enough, he could see the sea again. See his golden shore. See—

Snowy.

He slipped back into the forest, heading for the mountain. Near an ancient fallen tree, half cloaked in moss, he stopped. Something had been carved into the exposed wood – lines and dots like musical notes, etched deep and careful.

The boy traced them with a fingertip.

Cold. Even in the heat.

Someone else has been here.

The thought sent a shiver up his spine. He straightened and moved on.

A rustle overhead made him look.

Leaves trembled.

A flash of colour – vibrant feathers – and then faces peered down at him.

Monkeys.

Not like any he'd seen in books or at the zoo when he was five. Their fur was dark, but their heads and shoulders wore bright feathers like stolen crowns. And wings.

Flying monkeys.

Their eyes were clever and too intent. They seemed to watch the shells around his throat.

Then they moved. One dropped to a lower branch. Then another. Then three more, quick as rain.

The first reached for his necklace.

The boy laughed once – nervous, surprised – and lifted a hand as if to touch its feathers.

The monkey's fingers brushed his wrist. Delicate.

Then his neck. Two fingers hooked under the cord and tugged. Not playful. Testing.

A second monkey mirrored it from the other side, small hands fast, nails sharp. The cord tightened. The boy's breath caught.

His amusement vanished so quickly it felt like falling.

"They are mine!" he shouted. His voice cracked the green air. Loud. *Wrong.*

The monkeys startled, chattering in outrage. One released the cord; another screeched and leapt backwards. In a burst of feathers and leaves they scattered, flew away up into the canopy, disappearing as if they'd never been there.

The boy stood still, one hand at his throat, breathing hard. The cord had left a burning, raised line across his skin.

He kept walking. The jungle thinned at the base of the

mountain. Heat rolled off the dark rock in slow, heavy breaths. Steam hissed from narrow cracks. The ground felt warm through his soles.

"So mighty," he whispered, and the words came out respectful, as if he were speaking to something that could hear. To someone.

Then—

A voice. Low. Rough. Close enough to be real.

The boy stopped. Held his breath. Listened.

"...every breath I take disappears in the end," the voice murmured. "What have I become? Drowning in this darkness..."

He edged forward through the jungle's fringes until it ended abruptly, as though something had bitten a chunk out of it.

Not a clearing. A scar.

The undergrowth had been burned away in a wide, uneven circle. Blackened vines lay collapsed like dead rope. The air tasted faintly of old smoke.

At the far side, massive stones rose from the earth – ancient, moss-covered, bound by roots too thick to belong to any tree he knew. Between those stones, half-hidden, yawned a grotto: a mouth in the rock, dark and patient.

Inside, hunched over a small fire, sat a man.

He was tall – taller than any adult the boy knew – and his posture made him taller still, all angles and long bones folded tight as if he'd learnt how to make himself smaller. His hair was white and wild, sun-bleached and smoke-stained. His clothes might once have been fine, but now they were only burnt rags: charred hems, patched seams, sleeves cut short.

The boy crept forward without meaning to, chest low, feet careful, as if the jungle itself might hear him.

The fire was not a fire so much as a stubborn cluster of embers. A last red eye refusing to close.

And then the boy saw the man's neck.

A deep, old scar scored the right side of his neck, a jagged line running halfway to the collarbone, as though a claw had once tried to take his breath.

A small sound escaped the boy before he could swallow it.

The old man's head snapped up.

His eyes caught the embers' light – gold-flecked, bright in a way that didn't match the rest of him. Burning, but not cruel.

"You're staring," the man said. His voice was rough, scraped raw by long silence. But not unkind. "Either come in or leave. Don't hover like prey."

The boy froze.

"I won't hurt you," the man added, turning back to the fire as if the decision bored him. "Can't promise the same for whatever's behind you." A dry chuckle, like gravel. "Those things don't care much for manners."

The boy glanced back.

Nothing.

But the clicking sound came again – closer now, threaded through leaves like threatening teeth.

He stepped into the grotto.

Smoke and stone. Old ash. And something faintly sweet beneath it, like resin warmed by sun.

"I'm... I'm lost," he managed. "I'm looking for—"

"Snowy," the man said, as if finishing a sentence they'd both begun. "Let me guess – white polar bear."

The boy went cold.

The man's mouth twitched. "Sound carries on this island." He nudged the embers with a stick. They flared, then settled. "And you've been calling for it like it owes you."

The boy's throat tightened. Must have been in his sleep.

Up close, the man looked even stranger. Weathered skin. And beneath – a shimmer, almost, like heat above rock.

"Sit," the man said, not bothering to look up. "You're shaking like you've been rowing through grief."

The boy hesitated. *Trust.* In his head, Kofi's voice rose – not the words so much as the feeling.

He sat on a warm stone near the fire. The heat felt good. "Thank you," he said, because he didn't know what else to offer.

"Don't thank me yet." The man fed a strip of driftwood into the embers. Flame crawled up, cautious. "Haven't decided whether I'm keeping you."

"Keeping me?"

"Figure of speech," the old man said, too quickly, as if he'd forgotten how to speak around children. Then, softer: "Mostly."

He poked the fire, sending sparks spiralling up. The flames grew, and in their light, the boy saw the cave walls. They were covered in marks – scratches, burns that climbed the stone in arcing sweeps. The marks went up, across the ceiling, converging towards the cave's entrance like something had been trying to claw its way out.

"What are those?" the boy asked.

The old man didn't answer at once. He stared at the fire as if the flames were translating something he'd never learnt to read.

"Memories." His smile was sad. "Of every time I tried to fight it. Every time I clawed at the walls trying to stay what I was instead of becoming what I am." His eyes caught the firelight again, and for just a second, the young boy could swear they glowed. *Actually* glowed.

"I've lived a long time, my friend," the old man said. "Longer than any human should. And you know what I've learnt? The things that hurt most aren't the changes we surrender to. They're the changes we fight."

The boy swallowed. "I don't understand."

"You will." The old man rose with a stiffness that made pain visible. "Come. There's something you should see."

He led the boy deeper into shadow where the firelight didn't quite reach. There, scratched into the stone, was a drawing. Crude, but deliberate – like someone had returned to it again and again.

A man.

The same man with something breaking from his back – stubs, then lines, then the shape of wings forcing themselves into being.

Then wings fully spread. Burning.

Then nothing but ash and a small circle of light.

The boy's mouth went dry. "What is it?"

The man traced the lines with one finger, gentle as if touching a bruise.

"My story," he said. "So I couldn't lie to myself." He turned his head slightly. "I crossed a threshold once. A long time ago. Thought I was running towards something. Turns out I was running from it."

The boy's stomach dropped. "A door?"

The man's gaze sharpened – not surprised, but recognising. "Yes," he said, and there was heaviness in his words. "A door."

After a long silence, the boy asked: "You said you heard me calling for Snowy," the boy said, voice thin. "Do you know where it is?"

The man studied him with those gold-flecked eyes. "Are

you still waiting to be saved by that bear?"

The boy flinched as if struck.

"That's not—"

"Isn't it?" the old man asked. "You crossed your door. Left your room. Swam past where you were supposed to stop. Ran from a ship. Rowed until your hands split." He gestured to the boy's blistered palms without looking at them. "And you're here now, alone, still chasing a bear."

The boy's fists clenched. "Snowy's not—"

"Not what?" the man interrupted, and for the first time his voice rose, not loud, but sharp with something like impatience. "Not real? Not needed? Not a crutch?"

The boy's eyes burned. "Snowy is my friend."

The man's expression shifted, something like regret passing through it. He looked away as if the cave wall had suddenly become more interesting.

"Good," he said quietly. "Hold on to that. Friends are rare in places like this."

The boy's breath trembled. "Who are you?"

The man stared into the fire until the question stopped rattling.

"I had a name," he said. "I don't use it. Names are for people who belong somewhere." His mouth moved like it wanted to smile and couldn't find the shape. "I'm between things. Names don't stick in the middle."

He nodded towards the boy, once. "You are too."

"I'm not—" the boy began, then stopped because it was a lie and he was tired of lying. The tiredness lived in his bones now. "I'm just lost."

The man watched him with unsettling patience. "Lost, how?" he asked. "Lost your way? Or lost yourself?"

"Both," the boy whispered.

"Honest answer," the man said. "Good."

The fire hissed.

The boy's throat tightened again, and this time he couldn't outrun it. "I don't want to change," he said, and hated how small the words sounded. "If I change... if I become someone different, I will be gone."

The old man didn't speak. He didn't rush to comfort. He simply added another piece of wood and watched it catch. Flames climbed, bright and greedy.

"Say it," the old man said softly.

The boy's face went hot. "I don't want to forget my dad. Or my mum."

The words hung in the air like smoke.

The old man's eyes flicked shut for one beat. When they opened, they were gentler, but older.

"You won't," he said. "That isn't how it works." He touched his neck. "Grief changes a person. Marks them. But it doesn't erase what was loved." He looked at the boy. "It carries it forward, whether you want it to or not."

The boy clenched his jaw.

"And if I can't change?" he whispered. "If I'm too scared?"

"Then you do what I did," the man said. His voice went flat, like he was reciting a sentence he'd served. "You hide. You fight your own becoming until you're exhausted." He gestured at the claw marks on the walls. "You stay half-alive. Frozen between what you were and what you could be."

Wood split in the heat, spreading sparkles.

The boy wiped his cheeks hard.

The old man's gaze softened. "Surrender isn't defeat," he said. "It's acceptance." A pause. "It's trust."

Trust. Kofi's words. The boy's breath hitched.

The old man didn't move for a long time. Then he nodded

once.

"There's someone else you've lost recently," the old man said. "Someone who saved you. Yesterday, maybe. Or the day before. Time moves strange here."

The boy's hands clenched. "How do you know that?"

"I can see it on you. Fresh grief laid over old grief. They look different." The old man gestured at the boy's wrist. "And you've got rope burn. The kind you get from being cut free when you're in danger. Someone chose to save you instead of saving themselves."

The boy touched the mark without meaning to. "His name was Kofi."

"Was?"

"I don't know. I think – I think he's dead. The pirates attacked him and I fell and I couldn't see and..." The words tumbled out like they'd been waiting. "It's my fault. If I hadn't swum past the rocks, if I'd listened to Snowy, if I'd just—"

"Stop." The old man's voice was firm. "It's not your fault."

The boy's shoulders sagged. Then his face twisted, furious. "That doesn't help."

"I know," the man said, and there was no judgement in it. "You'll carry it anyway. That's what living does. We collect weight." He touched his scar again. "But here's the truth you don't want: weight doesn't stop you from changing. It goes with you."

The boy blinked. "Like... like the scars?"

"Yes." The old man smiled "Scars don't vanish. They become yours forever." A faint, strange smile. "Part of the wings."

"Wings," the boy echoed, and something inside him stirred.

"Metaphor," the old man said. "For letting go."

"Let go of what?"

"Control. Fear. The idea that change means death."

The boy felt something catching fire inside his chest. "I'm afraid. Of change. Of growing old. What if I become someone I don't know anymore? How do I know what..."

"You don't. That's what makes it terrifying. That's what makes it necessary."

The old man smiled, sad and knowing, quiet for a while. "It is hard," he finally said. "But you can't stay frozen as a child forever."

"Not *forever*."

"Living means changing. Always. That's what being alive *is*."

The old man added another piece of wood to the fire.

"You may lose memories. But your parents will live in you. In your bones. Your blood. Your voice." The old man smiled, and it transformed his weathered face. "Love changes everything. Even in death. Especially then."

For a while they sat in silence. The heat embraced them. The boy stared at the flame. It was hypnotic in the simplest way – always changing, never apologising.

"It's strange," the boy said hoarsely, "how fire can make a place feel like home. Even when it's just... this."

"Yes, fire has a way of doing that," replied the old man, watching the boy stirring the fire with a stick and playing with embers. "It's more than warmth it gives – it's the light, the hope."

Outside, the jungle shifted. Something moved. But it stayed beyond the scarred edges of the clearing, as if afraid.

The boy's eyelids began to drag. Smoke. Warmth. Feeling safe. The old man stood and disappeared into the shadows for a moment. When he returned, he draped his burnt coat over the boy's shoulders.

It smelt like smoke and time.

The boy's throat tightened again. "Will you be here when I wake up?"

The man's face went still. Not cold. Just... resigned.

"Perhaps," he said. "In a way."

The boy wanted to ask a hundred questions – about doors, about islands, about Snowy, about the glowing eyes and the claw marks and the wings that burned into the ash.

But his body betrayed him. Exhaustion pulled him down like tide.

The old man's voice lowered, almost a hum. "Sleep," he said. "You need it."

The boy let his eyes close.

For the first time since he'd left his room, for the first time since the lilies, the empty house, the dinner-table silence – he felt good.

"Don't be afraid," the old man said, very softly, as if to himself as much as to the boy. "You will grow old, while I shall stay the same."

And the boy slept.

He dreamt of heat. Not warmth – *heat*: the kind that turns breath into panic.

He was back in the cave. Only the cave was no longer dark. It was bright.

In the centre stood the old man. Inside the flames.

Fire wrapped his legs, his ribs, his arms. Cloth vanished first – paper-quick. Then the seams of him began to glow, red-gold, like metal in a forge.

"No," the boy gasped, scrambling backwards until stone dug into his spine. "Stop! You're..."

"Watch," the old man said. But it wasn't his voice now. It

was wind through flame. It was crackling wood. It was something ancient waking.

His back arched. Skin split – fine fractures, sudden and bright – like eggshell under pressure. Light poured through.

Then something forced itself out.

Wings. Not feather. Not scale. Fire made into shape: vast, curling at the edges like living flame. They unfolded wider than the cave could hold, and the air screamed with it.

The old man lifted his head.

His eyes were solid gold. The scar at his throat burned white, a single line of light.

"Don't be afraid," the voice said, and the words felt less spoken than *placed* inside the boy's chest.

The fire-being stepped towards the entrance. The cave couldn't hold it.

At the threshold it paused, turned, and looked back at the boy.

"Remember," it said. "When your time comes – don't fight."

The boy's throat tightened. "I don't know how."

"You'll know," the voice replied, already thinning into distance. "Trust the fire."

The wings flared. And the being rose – no effort, no struggle. Ascending. Burning. Becoming light itself.

Then he woke.

He was lying on bare rock at the forest's edge, the old man's coat draped over him. The stone beneath him was hot – too hot for morning. The air above shimmered. No cave. No fire. No old man.

The boy sat up. "Hello?"

Silence.

He looked down at his arms. At his chest. New marks: faint

burn-patterns, as if hot wire had been pressed against his skin. They didn't hurt. They simply... were.

His clothes bore the same marks – small scorch-patterns along the sleeves, the collar.

Fine grey ash dusted his shoulders. He brushed it off, confused.

"Hello?" he called again, louder. "Where are you?"

Nothing. Just jungle sounds. Birds. Wind.

Had he dreamt it? The cave, the fire, the old man talking about transformation – had any of it been real?

But the coat was real. Heavy. Warm. Smelling like smoke.

And the burns were real.

The boy stood. The coat slid from his shoulders and fell to the ground like an empty shell. He walked towards where the cave should have been. Searched the rockface, the boulders, the shadows.

Nothing. Just solid stone.

"I don't understand. Where did you go?"

The rocks gave no answer.

He searched for an hour, maybe more. Calling. Circling. Finding nothing.

Finally, frustrated and afraid, he returned to where he'd woken. That's when he saw it.

The coat was gone. In its place lay a pile of ash. Around it – two burnt shapes, fanning outward like spread wings.

The boy knelt. Touched the blackened stone. It was still warm.

He looked up. The air above wavered. Something flickered there – ash flakes, drifting, glowing faintly red-gold in the late morning light.

Feathers? No. Tiny pieces of light descending from somewhere high in the canopy.

The young boy caught one in his palm. It was warm. Weightless. Beautiful. Then it crumbled to nothing.

He searched for the source. But there was only sky. Only haze rising. And the sense that he'd missed something important.

Or had he?

The burns on his arms said he'd been there. Been close. Been touched by whatever this was.

But his memory was hazy. Fragmented. Like trying to recall a dream.

"Maybe it was a dream," he said aloud.

But dreams didn't leave wing-shaped scorch marks in stone. Dreams didn't leave coats behind. Dreams didn't burn you.

He looked at the wing marks one last time. Something had happened here. Something impossible.

He just didn't know what.

"I need to get up there," he told himself, and turned towards the dormant volcano.

He left the jungle's shade and studied the cliff face, searching for a way that wasn't sheer. When he found a seam in the rock – a broken spine of ledges and roots – he climbed.

It was hard, slow work. Fingers wedged into cracks. Knees finding purchase where they could. Each step was a bargain with gravity, each breath a small victory. As the air thinned, the world grew quieter.

Higher still, the canopy dropped away beneath drifting cloud. His heart hammered against his ribs. Moisture beaded on his skin and chilled in the wind. He climbed until the stone levelled in a plateau and the clouds parted.

Then he saw it. The endless, vast, indifferent ocean under a skin of mist. No familiar curve of the golden shore. No

Snowy. Just emptiness where hope should have been. An ocean of it.

He stood there, breath unsteady, disappointment rising like tidewater. For a moment it was as if the whole world had been a trick. No heights could show him a way back. The old man had been right, he realised. Some part of him had still been waiting to be saved.

"There's nothing wrong with looking for my friend," he muttered, but the words didn't land the way he wanted them to.

He turned away and began to descend.

He chose the far side – barren, unshaded, less steep – but the rock was loose, skittering beneath his feet. Every careful step down felt heavier than the climb. The mountain was silent again, only now it didn't steady him. It only reminded him how alone he was.

He kept moving anyway. One step, then another. He didn't know where the slope would take him. He only knew he couldn't stay up there, staring at a horizon that offered nothing back.

If Snowy was out there, he would have to find him on his own.

Even the wildest can be tamed.

The old man's words, *not* his. They came back with the taste of smoke. Maybe that was what this was: not taming the wild outside, but the wild inside. The part that wanted to bolt. The part that wanted to freeze time and call it safety.

By late afternoon he reached the shoreline again. The surf softened the ache in his feet, the familiar push and pull of water making the world feel whole again.

The longboat still lay where it had washed up, half-dried in the sun, waiting like a question that hadn't gone away.

He set to work.

He dragged driftwood and thin trunks from the tide line. Twigs. Vines. Strips of bark. He twisted them into rope until his palms burned. He lashed the pieces together, reinforcing the boat's ribs, widening its base, turning it into something closer to a raft – crude, stubborn, real.

His hands fell into a rhythm that quieted his thoughts. Loop. Pull. Tighten. Knot. Again.

When he finally stepped back, what he'd built was modest – barely enough for one small boy and a little luck. It was not a promise. It was a choice.

Yet when he hauled it into the shallows and felt it lift under him, pride rose, sharp and unfamiliar. Independence, too. A fierce, trembling thing.

He gathered what little he could find: fruits, juicy roots, leaves torn from the jungle. Then he climbed in. Took the oars. He didn't know where he was going. But he knew he was going. Terrified, but ready.

And for the first time in a long time, the weight in his chest shifted. Not gone. Just... different. Like grief turning from a stone into something he could carry. Something that could carry *him*.

He rowed until the jungle was just a green smudge shadowed by a dark smouldering mountain behind him. Until the world was water and sky and the steady bite of the oars. Until he was alone with nothing but a rope scar on his wrist and a memory of wings made of fire.

He rowed. Quiet. Alone.

But changed.

Chapter IV: The Singing Fairies

«Beneath the sky, through forests deep,
The boy climbed high the fiery steep.
And set his path, with hope in tow,
Driving his raft where wild winds blow.»

Three days at sea.

Maybe four. The boy had stopped counting.

The half-raft, half-longboat drifted on the surface of depth. The sun rose and fell. The ocean moved beneath him, breathing. Vast. Silent.

He lay flat on the wet logs, staring at the sky. In the silence, broken only by the gentle lapping of waves against the wood, he felt weightless, floating over the unknown. His lips were cracked. His throat felt like sand. But it wasn't thirst that kept him still.

It was the memory.

The old man burning. The dream. Wings spreading. Light consuming everything.

Don't be afraid.

The boy closed his eyes. Opened them. The sky was still there. Still blue. Still empty.

Was it real?

The healing rope and burn marks on his arms said yes. But his mind kept circling back to the same question: *Why show me that?*

The old man had talked about surrender.

When your time comes, don't fight.

"But what am I becoming?" The boy whispered to the empty sky.

The ocean didn't answer. Well, not truly. A plume of breath rose, a dark curve against the light, then vanished with a single sweep of tail into the depth. But that didn't count as an answer.

On the fourth night, or maybe the fifth, he saw stars.

Real stars. Not the painted-on kind from his bedroom ceiling. These were sharp and bright and impossibly far away, and looking at them made his chest ache.

His mother used to point out constellations. Make up stories about them. Her voice in the dark, warm and close: *That one's the Bear. See? Those stars make the body, and those make the head...*

He'd forgotten that.

When was the last time you thought about her laugh?

The boy pressed his palms against his eyes. Hard. Until colours bloomed behind his eyelids.

He wasn't crying. He was just... tired. That's all.

The half-raft drifted.

On the sixth day, a bird.

Small. White. Crying in that sharp, repetitive way that seabirds do.

The boy sat up so fast the longboat rocked. His head spun. His vision blurred. But the bird was real, circling overhead, screaming at the ocean.

Birds meant land.

He scanned the horizon. Nothing but water. White, briny mist. But there – a dark line, green, solid.

Land.

He grabbed the oar and paddled. His arms screamed. His shoulders burned. He didn't care.

The island grew. Trees. White sand. The sound of surf against shore.

When the wood scraped bottom, the boy fell more than climbed off it. His legs buckled. The sand was solid and impossible and real.

He crawled to the tree line. Found a thin stream. Drank.

The water tasted like minerals and earth and life. Mud and water. He drank until his throat hurt, then drank more.

Then he grabbed handfuls of pulpy roots and leaves, biting into them, sucking out their sweet juices, swallowing them half-chewed. Sickness and pleasure twisted together in his gut. As his stomach filled and exhaustion settled over him, warmth spread through his limbs. The birdsong, the far-off rush of water – all of it softened around him.

He collapsed onto the cold moss in the shade and let sleep take him. He couldn't remember ever feeling so full, so still.

He woke to singing.

Not human singing. Not bird singing. Something else.

The boy opened his eyes.

The air was alive with sound – high trills, bright warbles – and the scent of honey and spice. Swirls of rustling leaves danced in the sunbeams. The forest was brimming with light. Not sunlight, although that was there too, filtering through leaves. Smaller lights. Moving lights. From every hidden nook and cranny, flying gracefully through the air. Dozens of them. Hundreds. Floating, dancing, singing.

Fairies.

The boy sat up slowly, afraid to move too fast, afraid they'd vanish.

They were tiny. Smaller than his hand. Their wings blurred with motion, leaving trails of light in the air like threads. And they sang – high, clear notes that wove together into something that wasn't quite music and wasn't quite language but felt like both.

Beautiful.

One floated close to his face, hovering there, looking at him with bright, curious eyes, almost amused.

The boy held his breath.

The fairy touched his nose – one quick tap – then darted away, laughing. The sound was like bells.

More came. Circling. Curious.

"Hello," the boy tried.

They scattered at his voice, chittering in alarm. Then, cautiously, they drifted back.

The boy tried again. "I'm looking for someone. A white bear, called—"

The fairies scattered again. This time farther. Their song changed – confused, wary.

"Wait!" The boy stood. "Please. I need help. I need to find—"

But they were already gone, vanishing into the canopy like sparks from a fire.

The boy stood alone in the clearing, breathing hard.

Words didn't work.

They didn't understand words.

He tried countless times.

Drew pictures in the dirt – a bear shape, a boy shape, waves for the ocean. The fairies watched, curious, but didn't respond.

He tried different languages – the few words he knew in Spanish from school, some French his mother had taught him, even nonsense sounds hoping they'd mean something.

Nothing.

The fairies sang. Danced. Ignored his questions.

The boy sat down hard, frustrated. "How am I supposed to find Snowy if I can't even ask where he is?"

One fairy landed on his knee. Looked up at him with those too-bright eyes.

The boy tried again, slower. "Snowy. White bear. Do you know—"

The fairy sang a quick trill – three notes, *high-low-high* – then flew away.

The boy watched it go.

Three notes.

High-low-high.

He hummed them. Tentative. Uncertain.

High-low-high.

Three fairies stopped mid-flight. Turned. Looked at him.

The boy's heart jumped.

He hummed again. *High-low-high.*

More fairies came. Five. Ten. Twenty maybe. They circled him, singing back – not the same notes, but answering notes. Harmonising.

The boy laughed. Once. Surprised.

He tried a different pattern. *Low-high-low-high.*

The fairies responded immediately, their song weaving around his, adding layers, complexity, joy.

Not words.

Music.

The boy stood. Hummed. Whistled. The fairies danced around him, singing, their lights making patterns in the air.

And when the boy walked – still whistling, still humming – the fairies moved with him, lights circling and beckoning, leading him deeper into the forest. Showing him the way.

The fairies brought him to a clearing filled with exotic flowers and tall, red mushrooms. At the centre was an enormous mushroom, cloaked in moss and featuring windows and even a door. "This must be what you wanted to show me," the boy realised. "Thank you!" he said, even attempting to sing it. Although it was probably not the melody of gratitude. The fairies answered with bright, tinkling laughter as they darted into the branches. Carefully, the child approached the mushroom house, mindful not to disturb the peaceful, fragrant glade.

The mushroom-house was hollow inside, carved and shaped and filled with soft light that seemed to come from everywhere and nowhere. The entrance – a doorway made of wood, formed like two hands pressed together – was overwhelming.

The boy stood before it, uncertain – the air warm with the scent of sap and feather-dust.

"Come within, little wanderer." The voice was warm. Musical. Human.

The boy stepped inside. Cool air brushed his skin, rich with the earthy sweetness of the mushroom's flesh.

A lady of bright blue eyes and feathered grace sat on a

woven chair that seemed to grow from the floor itself. A Fairy Queen. She was tall – taller than the boy, though not by much. Her wings were different from the others'. Not blurred or iridescent, but plumed like a bird's, catching the light and breaking it into warm colours.

Her blue eyes were kind. Sad in a way he knew too well.

"Thou carriest the scent of far places, little wanderer. Far from home," she said.[1]

The boy's throat tightened. "Yes."

"What seekest thou so far?"[2]

"I'm looking for my friend. A white bear. Its name is Snowy. We got separated and I..." He stopped. "I don't know where it is."

The Fairy Queen was quiet for a long moment. "Sit," she said finally, gesturing to a cushion across from her.

The boy sat.

"Long hast thou walked in solitude," she said.[3] Not a question.

"No. Only a few days. Maybe a week. I don't know."

"Nay." She shook her head. "Longer than that."

The boy looked down at his hands.

The Fairy Queen leaned forward. "Loss clingeth to thee. Thy absence hath a shape – mother, father. Love."[4]

The words hit like a fist. Three months since his mother died. Six years since his father. The boy couldn't breathe.

"How...?"

"I see it in thee – the way thy form remembereth sorrow."[5]

---

[1] You carry the scent of distant places, little wanderer. Far from home.
[2] What are you searching for this far away?
[3] You've walked alone for a long time.
[4] Loss clings to you. Your absence has a shape – mother, father. Love.
[5] I can see it in you – the way your whole being remembers sorrow.

Her voice was unbearably gentle.

The boy's vision blurred. He wiped his eyes fast, angry at the tears.

"I am sorry," the Fairy Queen said.

"Everyone's sorry." The words came out harder than he meant. "But sorry doesn't bring her back."

"Nay. It doth not."[6]

They sat in silence.

"Grief humeth within thee – heavy and wordless," the Fairy Queen said finally.[7]

The boy didn't answer.

"It maketh us forget how to speak. We strive to bind it in words, yet grief is not wrought of speech. Nay – it is fashioned of absence, of weight, of the hollow where a presence should abide."[8]

She paused, the air tightening around her.

"Some things grow too vast for language."

The boy looked up at her.

"Thy mother," the Fairy Queen said softly. "Speak to me of her. Not her words, nor her tales. Tell me... the warmth she bore."[9]

"I don't – I don't know what you mean."

"Close thine eyes."[10]

The boy hesitated. Then closed them.

"Let the memory rise sans the snare of language. How she

---

[6] No. It doesn't.
[7] Grief hums inside you – heavy and without words.
[8] It makes us forget how to speak. We try to trap it in words, but grief isn't made of speech. No — it's made of absence, of weight, of the hollow where someone should be.
[9] Your mother. Tell me about her. Not her stories or her words. Tell me... the warmth she carried.
[10] Close your eyes.

made thee feel."[11]

The boy sat very still.

And there she was.

Not her face. Not her laugh. Just... the feeling of her. The warmth. The safety. The way the world drew close around her, gentle and sure, like nothing bad could really happen as long as she was there.

"That," whispered the Fairy Queen. "Aye... that feeling. That is the truth that lieth beneath all naming – beneath the din of words. And hard it is to keep."[12]

The boy opened his eyes. His cheeks were wet.

"Language is fair. Yet a lie it is as well. We use it to name things, to bind them, to make them smaller so that we may hold them. But certain things – love, grief, joy, fear – grow vast, too vast for naming. They dwell beneath all words, in that deep place where we dare not speak, but... feel."[13]

"Why are you telling me this?"

"Because thou seekest that which thou hast lost. And where thou goest next, words shall avail thee naught. The ancient beings thou shalt meet speak not as we do. They speak in elder tongues – languages of feeling and presence and truth." She touched his hand. "Thou canst not bargain with the ocean in words. Thou must hearken to the song of all things."[14]

---

[11] Let the memory rise without the trap of words. How she made you feel.

[12] That. Yes... that feeling. That's the truth beneath all naming – beneath the noise of words. And it's hard to hold on to.

[13] Language is beautiful – but it's a lie too. We use it to name things, to bind them, to make them small enough to hold. But certain things – love, grief, joy, fear – grow too vast for naming. They live beneath all words, in that deep place where we don't speak, but... feel.

[14] Because you're searching for what you've lost. And where you're going next, words won't help you. The ancient beings you'll meet

The boy looked back at the fairies swirling through the trees. "Is that what they taught me? With their whistling?"

The Fairy Queen smiled. "Aye. The creature thou dost seek speaketh this tongue with ease. If thou canst not hear the truth that lieth beneath its words, thou shalt hear only what thou expectest... not what thou needest."[15]

"What creature?"

"If thy white friend be anywhere, the Bear that dwelleth across the water, where the sun doth rise, shall know. Yet thou canst not question it as thou hast questioned me. It will not understand. It speaketh the elder way."[16]

"How will I know if I'm hearing right?"

"Even as thou knewest which notes to whistle, so shalt thou know this. Thou shalt feel it – in thy bones, in thy breath. Trust that feeling, child. Trust the wordless knowing. It shall save thy life more than once."[17]

"So... shall I sing to the eastern bear?"

The Fairy Queen laughed. "Nay. Thou speakest not to it. Thou standest in its presence even as thou once stoodst in thy mother's." She squeezed his hand. "Grief hath taught thee well – stilling thee, sharpening thine ear. Feeling is the tongue of

---

don't speak like we do. They speak in older tongues – languages of feeling, presence, and truth. [...] You cannot bargain with the ocean in sentences. You must learn to listen to the song of all things.

[15] Yes. The creature you seek speaks this language fluently. If you cannot hear the true meaning beneath its words, you will only hear what you expect [to hear]... not what you need [to hear].

[16] If your white friend is anywhere, the Bear that lives across the water, where the sun rises, will know. But you cannot question it the way you questioned me. It won't understand. It speaks the elder way.

[17] The same way you knew which notes to whistle, so you will know this. You'll feel it – in your bones, in your breath. Trust that feeling, child. Trust the wordless knowing. It will save your life more than once.

the elder beings. This is the oldest language."[18]

The boy didn't know what to say.

The Fairy Queen stood. "Thou wilt need something for the path."[19]

She moved to the back of the mushroom-house and returned with a length of wood. Smooth. Pale. Carved with symbols that seemed to shift in the light. And she also brought a small bundle wrapped in leaf-cloth.

"A wand," the boy said, looking at the wood.

"A branch. From the Singing Tree. It shall aid thee in the shaping of wood, in the bending of plants, in the fashioning of what thou hast need of." She held it out. "Yet it worketh only if thou askest sans words – if thou feelest thy need and lettest the wand answer. Press or command it, and it shall not heed thee."[20]

The boy took it. It was warm. Alive, almost.

"Take this loaf for the road," said the Fairy Queen, setting the bundle in his hands. "It is baked with the seeds of the Flower-of-a-Thousand-Dreams, gathered at the height of its dreaming. The path ahead is long, and thou art still but a child."[21]

"Thank you."

---

[18] No. You don't speak to it. You stand in its presence the way you once stood in your mother's. [...] Grief has taught you well – teaching you silence, sharpening your listening. Feeling is the language of the elder beings. This is the oldest language.

[19] You'll need something for the journey.

[20] A branch. From the Singing Tree. It will help you shape wood, bend plants, and make what you need. [...] But it only works if you ask without words – if you feel what you need and let the wand answer. Push it or command it, and it won't respond.

[21] Take this loaf for the road. [...] It is baked with seeds from the Flower-of-a-Thousand-Dreams, gathered at the height of its dreaming. The path ahead is long, and you are still only a child.

"Thank me not yet." The Fairy Queen's smile was sad. "The road ahead is shadowed. Ere thou findest the East Bear, thou must cross a river." [22]

"A river?"

"A Shadow-River." She touched his shoulder. "A mirror to thy soul. Fight it not. Name it not. Let it flow."[23]

"I don't understand."

"Thou shalt. If thou pass the river and the ocean, then shalt

---

[22] Don't thank me yet. [...] The road ahead is shadowed. Before you reach the East Bear, you must cross a river.

[23] A Shadow-River. [...] A mirror to your soul. Don't fight it. Don't name it. Let it flow."

thou find, at the sunrise forest's heart, the Great Tree where the East Bear dwelleth." She walked him to the door. The forest outside was bright, alive with fairy song. "Follow the lights. They know thy way."[24]

The boy wanted to kiss her hand. But the Fairy Queen leaned in, embracing him, hiding her tears as she held him tight. Then, she quickly dried her eyes and smiled, blessing his forehead with a kiss.

The boy stepped outside. Turned back. "Will I see you again?"

Amber touched the Fairy Queen's blue eyes – there, then gone, like a flame brushing in from tomorrow. "Only in thy dreams," she whispered, more to herself than to him. Then, aloud: "Perchance our paths shall cross again. Yet more important – seek thy balance."[25]

Twilight made the forest strange.

The day-fairies – bright voices, quick laughter – had gone quiet as if someone had closed a book mid-sentence. In their place, other shapes moved between the trunks: translucent, slower, edged in shadow. Their wings were the colour of ash. Their eyes caught the last light and turned it silver. When they sang, it was low and mourning, like a lullaby sung to something that would not wake.

---

[24] You will. If you pass the river and the ocean, then you'll find, at the eastern forest's heart, the Great Tree where the East Bear lives. [...] Follow the lights. They know your way.

[25] Only in your dreams. [...] Perhaps our paths will cross again. But more importantly – learn to find your balance.

The boy walked with care, the wand balanced in his hand like a fragile promise.

The path twisted. Narrowed. Brambles leaned in. The air cooled, damp with leaf-rot and dusk. With every step the light thinned, and the shadows gained weight.

Then he heard it.

Water.

Not a trickle. Not a stream. A rush – wide and fast.

He pushed through a veil of fern and found a river cutting the world in two.

It was black, not because it reflected the sky, but because it reflected nothing at all. Mist rose from its skin in slow breaths. The current worried at the mist like something cold hunting for shape. He couldn't see the far bank; it might have been yards away or miles. It might not have existed.

"I have to cross," he said, and his voice sounded too small for that water.

The river did not answer.

The boy held up the wand. *Bridge,* he thought. *Planks. Rope. Something solid.*

The wand *warmed* – then nothing.

He tried again, fingers tightening with the desperation of a fall.

Still nothing.

A laugh came from the river. Then a voice rose from dark – mature, somehow familiar. "Are you lost, boy?"

"Who are you?"

"The more of me there is, the less you see. Who do you think I am?"

Focus, he thought. He clenched his teeth. *Bridge. I need a bridge. Make it. Now.*

The wand stayed warm, patient – and inert.

"You cannot do it, can you?" the older voice hissed. The mist shivered. The black water heaved as if something beneath it had turned over. "You pretend you're brave. But you're a child clutching a stick, hoping it will save you."

"I'm not," the boy said through his teeth.

"You are."

The river surged, slapping the bank.

"You think a bridge will appear just because you want it. You think wanting is enough."

"Stop it."

"You can't cross this." The voice rose, cold and furious. "Look at me! You can't even face me." And it laughed.

He shook his head. "You're not real."

The voice laughed even more. The river laughed. A sound like stones grinding under deep water.

"I am every thought you push away. I am every truth you refuse to name. I am the part of you that knows you will fail." And then, with a mocking imitation, "I'm not real. Ha!"

"Shut up."

"Make me."

The current lunged at the bank, black, cold water clawing at his feet. The boy jerked, pulling back.

"If you cannot command yourself," the river voice said, low and venomous, "how will you command magic?"

That's right, the boy realised. *I can't command it.* And the word clicked, the Fairy Queen's voice reaching him as if through a dream: *"Push it or command it, and it won't respond. It only works if you ask without words."*

The boy lowered the wand. Took a breath.

Stopped trying to think.

Just... felt.

I need to cross. I need to reach the other side.

The wand pulsed once.

The laugh stopped. Silence fell; and it felt worse than the voice that had come before. The mist tightened, drawing close around his ankles.

"There," the voice murmured, softer, darker, edged like broken glass. "That is the truth you fear. Not me. Yourself."

But he stopped listening. His heart was singing.

In the water, roots began to rise. Not a bridge. A path. Knotted roots breaking the surface, forming stepping stones across the current.

The voice fell quiet.

The boy stared. Then stepped onto the first root.

It held.

He crossed. Slowly. Carefully. The river rushed past, cold and angry, but the roots stayed firm.

Halfway across, he saw it.

A figure. Standing on a root ahead of him.

It looked like...

Him.

Same height. Same build. Same clothes.

But wrong. The eyes were hollowed out, as if someone had scooped the light away. The smile didn't reach anywhere. It sat on the face like a mask left behind after a fire.

The sight hit him like a blow. The boy looked down, away from those hollow eyes.

"Hello," it said, in that distorted older voice.

The boy stopped abruptly; the river's spray dotted his lips. He tasted iron and cold.

"Who are you?" he asked, though his chest already knew.

The shadow-boy tilted its head, mirroring him perfectly. "You know who I am."

"No, I—"

"Look at me, boy. I'm the part you won't look at." The shadow's voice stayed gentle, which somehow made it worse. "The part that whispers when you're trying to be brave."

The boy's fingers tightened around the wand until his knuckles ached.

"I'm your fear that they're really gone. You almost forgot your father's warmth, now your mother's," the shadow continued, stepping closer with the easy balance of something that belonged on this river. "You swam beyond the stones. And now Kofi is dead. That changed you." Almost admirative, sardonic. "You have grown. They wouldn't recognise you anymore." A pause, soft as mist. "Your fear that one day you'll forget them completely – and it won't even hurt."

"That's not true," the boy said. He heard how thin it sounded.

The shadow smiled. "Isn't it?"

"No. I—" He stopped. Something inside him flinched, and in that flinch his mother's voice arrived, so clear it hurt: *Don't lie, sweetheart. Not to yourself.*

His mouth opened. Closed.

"Maybe," he admitted, and the word tasted like salt. "I don't know."

The shadow's smile widened – empty, pleased. "At least you're honest."

"What do you want?" the boy asked. His heart was clawing against ribs, but he didn't step back.

"To stop you." The shadow's gaze flicked past him, back to where the boy had come from. "To keep you here. To fight you, if I must."

"Why?"

The shadow straightened, its edges trembling with the current.

"You think you can cross," it said, voice low and tight. "You think you can leave me behind."

He tightened his grip on the wand. "I have to."

The shadow's mouth curled – not a smile, but the idea of one. "You can't leave what you are." A ripple of black water curled around the roots at the boy's feet. "You don't outrun what you refuse to face."

"I'm not running."

"You are," the shadow hissed. "You run from fear. From truth. From yourself. Why did you go through that door?"

That is... true. The boy sighed.

"Of course it's true," the shadow said, as if hearing his thoughts. "Cross me?" it breathed the words out. "You can't even look at me.

"But fear no more," said the shadow with the voice of the river. "I'm here to fight for you, for her. To protect you." It spread its hands as if offering a gift. "In this place, you can stay small," it said. "It's magic, you know? Never grow old. And never forget them as they were. Your father's strength. Your mother's warmth."

The boy's breath hitched. Tears slid hot against the cold mist.

The shadow stepped closer. Its voice softened, coaxing. "No... don't cry. Just... stay." The shadow lifted its chin. "Stay in fairyland. Stop trying. No more becoming."

The boy shook his head once – small. Then again, harder, as if shaking loose a net.

"I can't."

The shadow blinked, almost curious. "Why not?"

"Because..." The boy's voice broke and he hated it, but he kept going. "Because they wouldn't want that."

He wiped his face with the back of his wrist, smearing mist

and tears together. He lifted his chin, forcing himself to meet those hollow eyes.

"They'd want me to live," he said. "To grow. To be here." His breath shuddered. "Even if it hurts. Even if I change. Even if I become someone diff—"

But the shadow didn't wait for him to finish. It lunged.

The water-spectre struck him hard, pushing him back – its touch unsettlingly familiar, like the echo of a sibling's grip.

He wrestled against it, and the shadow answered him with equal force.

Their struggle was fierce and close, every hold and wrench a wordless argument, every gasp a confession.

It was a fight turned inwards – desire pulling him forward, instinct dragging him back, the river forcing him to wrestle with himself.

The clash tightened, water and boy locked in a single breath.

The spectre shoved him down; he pushed back harder.

Neither gained ground.

Then something in him cracked – not with pain, but with clarity.

"I see you," he gasped.

The spectre froze.

"I see what you are."

The water loosened its grip, as if the river itself exhaled. The shadow's face – his face – wavered, losing its edges.

"At last," it whispered, not angry now, but tired. "Name me."

"You are me who never left. Who never changed. And I'm scared," the boy said, and the words came faster now, like truth finally finding a door. "We're both scared. I'm terrified I'll forget what they sounded like. What they looked like. The way they made me feel. And you, you are in pain. Never able to forget. Not her singing, not him smiling, but their death. For me, nighty-one days of growing apart, for you – a river of pain.

"But you are wrong. Grief doesn't erase what was loved." Old man's words. The boy's fingers loosened slightly around the wand. "We were not going to lose them."

The shadow's smile twitched, uncertain. "Do you really believe that?" it asked.

The boy hesitated. The honest answer rose, trembling. "I want to."

"That's not the same thing."

"I know." He drew a breath that hurt, and held it anyway. "But maybe wanting to believe is enough. For now."

The wand warmed again – steady, approving – like a hand placed gently between his shoulders. His father's memory.

The roots beneath his feet tightened, as if listening.

The boy looked past the shadow, into the mist where the far bank waited unseen.

Then he took one careful step forward.

"Wait," the shadow called.

The boy turned.

"You can't outrun me, you know. I'm part of you. I'll always be here. The doubt. The fear. The grief."

"I know."

"Good." The shadow reached out. Its hand was cold, insubstantial. But when it touched his leg, he felt something – a burning sensation, sharp and brief.

Then the shadow dissolved. Became mist. Became nothing.

The boy looked down at his foot.

A small mark. Red. Like a scar.

Not a wound. A reminder.

He crossed the rest of the river alone.

On the far bank, dawn was breaking.

The boy collapsed on moss, exhausted.

He'd made it.

He looked at the scar on his foot. Touched it gently.

The shadow was right. It would always be part of him. The fear, the doubt, the grief. He couldn't outrun it. Couldn't fight it. Couldn't explain it away with words.

He could only carry it.

And maybe – maybe that was okay.

The boy stood. The forest on this side was brighter. Warmer. The fairy songs were different here – higher, clearer, full of joy.

He walked.

And as he walked, he thought about them. His mother. His father. Not his words. Not her voice. Just the feeling of them.

The love.

It was still there. Inside him. Part of him.

Changed, yes. Different than when they were alive. But not gone.

Never gone. Just transformed.

He stopped for a while and fell asleep. A deep dark sleep, yet full of warmth, with wings and songs.

A cry woke him up. Thin and urgent, as wind through reeds. Repetitive. Desperate. It was close, coming from a mushroom marsh. The wand warmed in his hand. The marsh deepened into shadow. Mushrooms leaned like listening giants. He thought of a narrow bridge of light. And the bridge grew from twigs, old wood and leaves. Not of light, but green.

He stepped on the creaking wood, and allowed the sound to carry him forward. In a hollow between swollen caps, he found them – tiny chicks struggling in the hungry mud, their breaths faint, their bodies sinking inch by inch. Something in him tightened. He stepped off the bridge and knelt.

The mud clung greedily, but he freed the young birds one by one, their fragile weight barely more than a handful of feathers. He carried them in his arms back to the river's edge, where the water ran clear and cold, and washed the mire from their down.

As the river touched them, a shimmer stirred beneath the grime. Gold. Then scarlet. Then a flicker of blue along a crest. The boy blinked, unsure if the light came from the water or

from the birds themselves.

But with each gentle stroke of water the glow strengthened. The feathers brightened. The air warmed.

A spark leapt. Then another.

And then the sun broke through the canopy. The chicks trembled. Not with fear. With heat.

Another spark leapt, bright enough to sting his eyes.

He drew in a breath. Not ordinary birds. Not even close.

Fire stirred inside their tiny bodies, stretching, waking, as if his hands had given it permission. As if they had been waiting – not for magic, but for someone gentle enough to lift them free. The chicks shook off the last clinging drops, and flew from his open arms, wings catching the light in a burst of colour. With a chorus of cries, they rose into the sky, feathers trailing behind them like falling stars.

Phoenix youth. The truth settled over him like light. And all they had needed was a hand willing to save them.

The boy watched them vanish into the blue and felt a smile rise unbidden. Grief lingered at the edges. His father's kindness. His mother's smile. Still there, steady as embers, ready when he needed them most.

The wand in his hand pulsed in warmth. He didn't know where Snowy was. Didn't know if the East Bear would help him.

But he knew he'd changed. That was true.

Learnt to communicate beneath words. Learnt to carry grief instead of fight it. Learnt that some truths are too big for language.

And that there was always hope. Even if from a passing stranger.

He was ready.

Ready to meet the East Bear. Ready to continue the

journey. Ready to become whoever he needed to become. Even if it scared him. Especially if it scared him.

The boy walked towards the eastern shore. And for the first time in a long time, he didn't feel alone. The grief was still there. The fear was still there. The shadow was still there, marked on his foot like a promise.

But so was love. So was hope. So was the quiet, wordless truth that he would survive this. All of it.

He kept walking.

The coast appeared through the trees – white sand, blue water, morning light making everything gold.

The boy stood at the forest's edge. The ocean stretched before him. Endless. Beautiful. Terrifying in its depths.

He raised the wand. Didn't think. Just felt.

I need to cross. I need to reach the East.

The wand warmed.

Driftwood rose from the beach. Vines unwound from trees. Branches bent and twisted, weaving themselves together without his touch, responding to need instead of command.

A raft formed before him. Stronger than the one he'd built before. More elegant. Real.

Magic, yes. But magic that answered to feeling, not force. The boy climbed aboard. Picked up the oars the wand had shaped.

The ocean waited.

He pushed off from shore, rowing towards the East Bear, towards whatever truth waited on the other side of words.

Behind him, the fairy forest sang its wordless song.

And the boy understood it perfectly.

Chapter V: The Brief Encounter

«Twixt starlit skies and sea's deep sigh,
Lone heart to faerie tune doth fly.
Unto the Queen his soul revealed,
By mystic touch, his fate is sealed.»

In the eastern waters, where old whispers clung to the waves, the boy sailed his raft into a sea that did not want him.

The storm found him fast.

Waves rose like walls, then fell away into bottomless troughs. The raft bucked and shuddered. Spray slapped his face raw. He clung to the timber until his fingers cramped, whispering prayers to the wind.

When the next wave reared higher than the rest, he shut his eyes and remembered the Fairy Queen.

Not the warning. The lesson beneath it.

He lifted the wand, driven by nothing but need.

Shelter.

A filament of light unwound from the wood and drew itself around him. The raft shuddered, a low groan rising from its frame as if something inside it had woken. Stems bent. Roots wove. The space around him tightened. And the raft folded in on itself, becoming a sphere that sealed shut with a soft, irrevocable click around the boy.

Inside, the sea became a muffled fist. The air smelt of wet wood and salt. Darkness pressed close.

For a few heartbeats the sphere held.

Then water began to find its way in – cold needles through seams, trickling at first, then slipping in steady threads. The boy hugged his knees, listening to the timber complain.

Hold, he thought. Not to the wand. Not to the sea.

Just hold.

A pressure touched the sphere.

Not a wave. Not wind.

Something vast, moving beneath.

A sulphurous reek slipped through the wood. The sea heaved against the intruder, its surface breaking open with a roar.

The sphere jerked sideways, scraped – wood creaking under strain. The boy's head struck the inner wall. Stars burst behind his eyes.

Another pressure – closer, heavier – like the world trying

to bite down.

The sphere shuddered, and the water surged around his ankles. The darkness fractured with the wet clicks and the far, strangled groan of a throat.

He could not see the creature. But he could feel it: teeth, or stone, or the inside curve of something alive. The air turned thick with a deep, briny stink – old kelp and rot and the metal tang of the abyss.

The battered sphere bobbed in a steady rhythm, the slap of waves betraying a fast current.

It was not drifting anymore.

It was being carried.

A sudden weightlessness swept through him as the beast hurled itself in wild arcs, plunging into the depths and breaching the surface in a frenzy to be rid of its unwelcome burden. The rapid swings of descent and ascent left him reeling, clinging to the sphere's inner shell. Then, as abruptly as it began, the convulsions stopped, and a tense stillness settled as the creature slipped back into the deep.

The wand glimmered – weak, trembling. Just a smear of light trying and failing to hold back the dark.

And the water kept rising.

Ankle-deep. Shin. Knee.

He pressed against the curved wall, searching for height that wasn't there. The space hugged him tight. His breath came fast and sharp, loud in the cramped dark.

Waist-deep.

The wand... The thought flared. *Force the sphere wider. Push the water out. Make—*

Press or command it, and it shall not heed thee. The Fairy Queen's words struck clean as a slap.

No. Force was useless here. The wand answered only

feeling. And all he could feel was terror.

The water licked his ribs. Then climbed.

"Snowy!" he shouted into the dark. His voice cracked on the name. "Snowy, please!"

Nothing answered.

Only the steady, indifferent rise.

Neck-deep.

He tipped his head back, mouth open, drinking the last slice of air as if it could last. A few more inches. That was all.

His fingers found the wand – slick, slipping, suddenly too small to matter.

What good was magic against drowning?

What good was anything?

The water reached his chin.

And something inside him split open.

He was going to die.

Not maybe. Not if.

Here. Now.

In the dark. Alone – swallowed by the same ocean that had swallowed his mother's ashes three months ago.

Salt stung his lips, and for a second it was *that* salt again: the day the wind took her, the day the adults said words that didn't fit in his mouth.

The water touched his mouth.

He dragged in one last breath. Lifted his face.

The water covered his nose.

This is it.

And then—

A flash. A terrible, perfect clarity.

This is where she went.

Not into waves. Not into earth.

Into this.

This cold, crushing nothing where breath failed and light vanished and everything stopped.

She had gone into the dark and hadn't come back. Like his father did before her.

And now he was following.

The water closed over him.

His lungs screamed. His body thrashed – instinct, panic, animal terror—

Air. Air.

Stop.

He forced himself still.

I can't fight. Not this. I can't—

Another flash – his mother's last breath in the room where no one knew what to do with their hands.

A blow to the chest.

Is this what you felt?

This drop? This quiet?

His thoughts scattered, wild, tumbling.

I'm sorry.

I should've been there.

I was scared.

I didn't understand.

His chest burned. Spots burst across his vision.

I'm here.

Drowning. In the dark.

With you.

The terror cracked. Loosened. Slipped away like a hand releasing its grip.

I'm afraid. But I'm done fighting it.

He let go.

Not of life.

Of resistance.

Light. Struggle. Bargaining. The frantic, furious *no*—

All of it drifting from him like silt in a current.

This is death. This is the void. The drop.

And still, he remained.

Ninety-one days. Ninety-one mornings waking to silence. Ninety-one nights in the cold. Six years before that.

He had been drowning on dry land.

He had survived that.

The water held him. The dark held him. His body still clawed for air with a violence that shook his bones... but the terror—

The terror was gone.

I surrender.

He exhaled. Bubbles rose, slow and silver, drifting towards a surface he could no longer feel.

He closed his eyes and held the emptiness in his chest – the ache, the void – for one more second.

And another.

In that stillness, in that depth, something shifted.

Not gently.

Fast.

The beast holding him moved with force, surging upwards in a rush, striking the surface like a fist against air.

The water trembled. *Courage is not the quenching of fear, but the acceptance of it.* Snowy's words sparked through the child's mind. The dark flexed.

The wand in his hand warmed, a pulse answering his own.

The shelter around him shuddered. Timber softened, grain loosening as if it could breathe.

Seams opened – not breaking.

Unclenching.

Water poured out through the gaps. Air – salt-thick, rancid

– rushed in.

The boy gasped, coughed, dragged breath into his burning lungs. Cold slapped his skin. The world lurched.

But he was breathing.

Alive.

Yet not free.

Through the cracks in the sphere, he saw: an immense maw, edged with ivory spires, rhythmically opening to reveal the tempestuous sea, then closing to shroud him in darkness.

The sphere, tangled in seaweed and wedged between jagged spires deep in the cavernous curve of flesh, was battered by saltwater spray and wind.

Not a shark.

Not a beast.

A leviathan – ancient as the stories, vast enough to make the ocean feel like skin.

He was in its mouth.

The water stung his eyes. The salt burned his lips.

Creaking wood and the sour reek of rotting fish crowded his senses.

Encased in the leviathan, he felt his smallness – a flicker of life inside an ocean giant.

As his eyes adjusted, he saw other captives: fish of every kind, from anchovies to tuna, floundering between the spires and the tongue's ridged grooves.

He reached out. His fingertips brushed the smooth, cold eye of a fish beside him. Panic radiated off it – so sharp his mind gave it words.

"We are both lost souls, facing our oblivion," he whispered as the creature thrashed in its final moments.

Did it fear death?

Will I ever see the sun again?

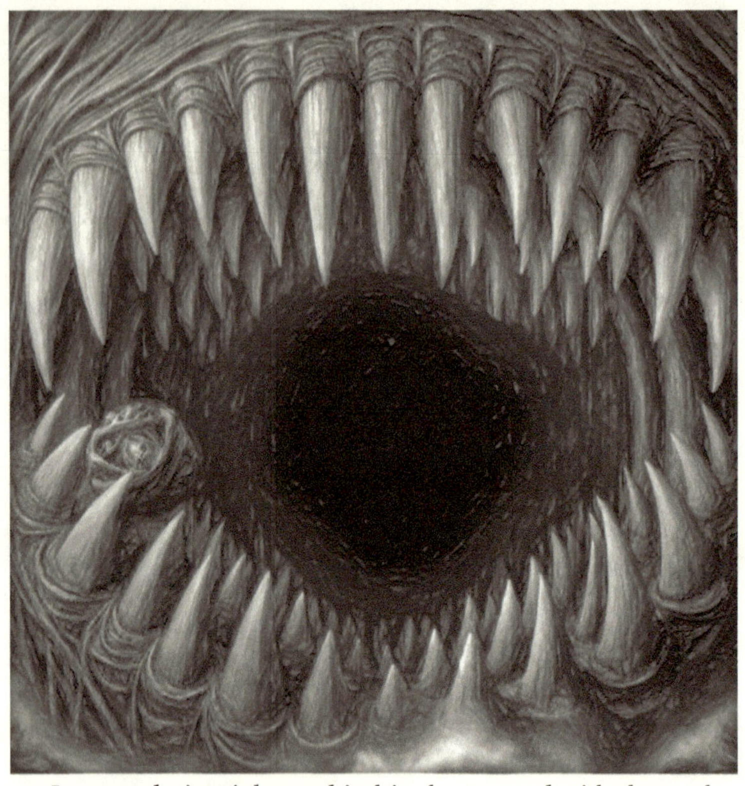

Love and pity tightened in his chest – and with them, the sharp truth of how small he was.

The leviathan moved again. Not in fury. Just... moved, as if it had made a decision.

The boy felt the shift – the massive body turning slowly, diving, then rising. And then he sensed it: the leviathan's pain. Not in words, but in its rhythm. It wasn't trying to kill him. It was suffering. *A language beyond speech.* The fairies had prepared him for this, though he hadn't known it then.

Water roiled in. His instinct snapped the wood back into place, sealing him inside the shell. The sphere shook as the waves churned violently around it. Again. And again.

Pressure eased. Then the sphere finally bobbed loose between teeth, slipping out. Not violently. Almost gently. The way you might spit out a seed.

The boy felt weightless for a moment – suspended. Then the sphere broke the surface with a gasp of displaced air. He didn't move. Couldn't. His lungs burned. His chest convulsed. His body decided to live without asking permission, coughing up water, dragging in air, refusing death even though his mind had accepted it.

He lay there, half-drowned, gasping, alive.

The sphere rocked gently on the waves.

Behind him – already sinking, already becoming myth again – the leviathan descended. He felt it in the currents pulling. In his heart.

It hadn't killed him.

It had let him go.

Or maybe it had never wanted him. Maybe he was only caught – trapped in the wrong place – and the ocean, at last, had returned what was not its own.

The way grief eventually releases you.

Not because you conquered it.

Because you stopped trying to.

The boy touched the wand. It was warm.

He didn't command.

He simply thought: *I need to see.*

The wood around him shifted, stirred by understanding. Magic wasn't control. It was release. The last curled edges of the sphere fell away, becoming raft again – stems flattening, roots withdrawing like fingers uncurling.

Daylight spilled over him. Pale, stubborn, cold.

He lay on the timber and stared at the sky, breathing.

He thought of the leviathan, the ancient beast that had

revealed the depths of his strength. He had faced the abyss, both within and without. But the void wasn't where they went, he realised.

It was what they left behind.

He pushed himself upright. His limbs trembled with exhaustion.

"Snowy," he whispered to the empty horizon. "I think I died. Or... I let myself die. And I'm still here."

The sea lapped softly at the raft, its slow, patient breathing pretending it had never tried to take him under. The sky stayed a clear, indifferent blue.

But something inside him had shifted.

He pressed a hand to his chest. His heart beat slow and steady, no longer trying to outrun the sentence.

They're gone. They're not coming back.

For ninety-one days he had circled that truth like a cliff edge.

Now he stepped onto it.

It held.

It didn't destroy him.

It simply existed – an absence that would never close. Still, it would not drown him.

He looked east, where the sun was lifting itself out of the water covered by clouds.

Towards the East Bear.

A flicker of motion caught his eye: dolphins slicing through the surface in silver arcs, chasing a scatter of fish. Wild, indifferent and alive, close enough to touch.

"And I nearly missed it," he said with a small smile.

Cold air brushed his skin.

Trust your feelings. Listen to your heart, the Fairy Queen had said. Now he understood it.

His parents were dead. That would never change.

But he was alive.

And he could carry them forward – not as a wound, but as memory.

As love.

He set the oars shaped by the wand and began to row towards the sunrise, towards whatever waited beyond these deep waters. Beyond the thinning gloom, the sun kept pace with him – steady, quiet, as if acknowledging his presence as the simplest truth.

He had faced the darkness and lived.

Now he was ready to begin again.

Chapter VI: The Enchanted Forest

«In treacherous depths, a boy's courage swells,
Against the storm, with magic spells.
From dark to light, his fears dispel,
A seeker's heart, the sea to quell.»

Fourteen days after the leviathan, the boy reached land, two days after the last of the fairy water had run off.

The shore was cold. Silt, leaves, scarce crab shells and fish scales. Real.

He knelt and pressed his palms flat against it, feeling the ground hold him. Solid. Unmoving.

For a moment he just breathed.

I'm here. Still here.

Behind him, the ocean whispered against the beach – patient, unconcerned, already forgetting him. Ahead, a forest rose like a wall of green, its canopy so thick the sunlight barely reached the ground.

East. The Fairy Queen said east.

The boy stood. His legs trembled – not from fear, but from fourteen days of rowing. His hands were blistered. His lips tasted like salt.

But he'd made it.

He touched the wand at his belt. It was warm. Humming, almost. Like it recognised something in the air.

The East Bear lives in the Great Tree, the Queen had said. *At the forest's heart.*

The boy walked towards the trees.

One step past the tree line and the world changed. The air turned cool. Damp. Thick with the smell of moss and rot and something sweet he couldn't name.

Light fell in shafts through the canopy, painting the ground in stripes. Birds called from somewhere high above. Insects hummed. Leaves rustled with movement he couldn't see. He quenched his thirst with dew gathered on the broad leaves of the undergrowth.

The boy walked carefully, watching where he stepped.

The wand pulled. Not hard. Not yanking. Just... a suggestion. Like a hand on his shoulder, guiding him left instead of right.

He followed it.

A tremor of wings brushed the canopy, spiralling through the leaves. Chirps and flickers in the ferns fled from his shadow. Something tiny rustled in the moss. Sound and breath rose around him as one.

As he walked, the trees grew taller. Thicker. Their trunks were wide as houses, their roots like serpents coiling over the ground. Vines hung from branches. Flowers bloomed in impossible colours – blue so bright it hurt to look at, red like fresh blood, yellow that glowed in the shadows.

Beautiful.

But something was wrong now.

The boy stopped.

He'd been walking for an hour, maybe more. And he'd just realised: every tree on his left was alive. Green leaves. Bright flowers. Birds nesting in the branches.

Every tree on his right stood dried and grey, neither rotting nor fallen – simply stilled. Scarred branches caught the sun; ash-dull leaves cast broken light across the ground. Each limb twisted upwards, fingers of wood bent and splintered. Fungi softened the fallen; russet and bronze moss drew life from decay. Little creatures nosed through the underbrush, a quiet stream of movement threading the ruin.

The boy turned in a slow circle.

The forest was split.

Left: life. Right: death.

A perfect line down the middle, like someone had drawn it with a blade.

He touched the nearest grey tree. The bark was cold. Hard as stone.

Then he touched a living tree.

Warm. Soft. Breathing, almost.

What happened here?

The wand pulled harder now. Urgent.

The boy followed.

He found the tortoise in a clearing where the split was clearest.

Half the glade was green. Grass. Flowers. Butterflies drifting through shafts of golden light.

Half was grey. Ash. Stumps. The ground cracked and barren.

And in the centre, straddling the line between life and death, lay the tortoise.

Its shell was massive. Dark gold. Cracked down the middle like someone had struck it with an axe.

The boy approached slowly.

The tortoise was dead. Had been for a long time. But something about it felt... wrong. The cracks in its shell didn't look like damage. They looked deliberate. Carved.

He knelt beside it.

The left half of the shell – the side in the living forest – was covered in moss. Green and thriving. Small flowers grew from the cracks, their roots digging into the dead creature's back.

The right half – the side in the dead forest – was bare. Grey. Covered in frost that shouldn't exist in the warm air.

This tortoise died on the border, the boy realised – as though the seam between these halves would not allow life. He traced the fissure with his fingers.

The moment his fingers brushed the shell, the world tilted. A vision flared in his mind.

Two bears – brothers – stood face to face in a clearing.

One was dark-golden, bright, its fur catching sunlight like honey.

The other was pale as an angel, its coat swallowing light like ash.

Between them stood a deep-rooted tree, with bark ridged like old stone. Sacred.

"The humans are coming," said the golden bear. Its voice was

warm, tired. "We cannot stop them. We should teach them. Guide them. Help them live with the forest instead of against it."

"No." The white bear's voice was cold. Final. "We drive them out. Before they destroy everything. Before they take what is not theirs."

"They're already here."

"Then we make them leave."

"Brother—"

"Do not call me that."

The white bear turned away, walking towards the sunset.

Shadow spread beneath its steps, the forest withering as if the land itself recoiled under the bear's breath.

The golden bear remained, watching its brother vanish into dark.

"I am sorry," it whispered to the empty clearing.

Then it walked towards the sunrise.

Light bloomed in its footprints, flowers rising where it passed.

Behind them, the ancient tree cracked.

Split like a wound.

The boy gasped and pulled his hand back, stumbling to the ground beside a half-buried, weathered stone. Beneath the moss, something shimmered.

His hand moved before he realised it had. He had barely touched the stone when runes flared to life – verses. They warmed, just enough to sting. Each mark rose with a different tune, threading itself into melodies that shaped into words inside his mind.

"As the day gives way to night," he whispered, "the faithful bird tends the fading light, cradling its warmth within the darkness of the nest. In our darkest hour, we too seek the healing within."

And the verses kept unfurling beyond the ones he could speak. The final lines, traced in ash, refused to settle into meaning. They hovered at the edge of sense – not quite words, not quite song – a melody he almost recognised but could not follow. He reached for their meaning, but they slipped away like mist, leaving only the ache of something important just beyond his grasp.

As he breathed the last verse, a sharp dizziness rolled through him, as if the forest had taken payment. The stone became silent again. Ordinary.

The clearing was just a clearing again. The tortoise just a corpse.

The boy stood. His hands were shaking.

He looked at the forest: bark split and blackened; branches hooked like claws; flowers recoiling from the ash, their gapped mouths lined with thorns. It was split, broken, held in balance only because both sides refused to give ground. He could feel it now. *They split the forest. And what couldn't choose a side – died.*

Water cut through it all, unbroken, refusing the line the forest obeyed. He followed the sound until the hidden river slid into view, clear as glass against the ruin. He knelt, cupped his hands, drank. Cold spread through his chest, easing the ache in his limbs. His breath slowed. When he stood again, the path behind him felt distant, already closing.

He pulled some fruit and ate it. Then he split the rest and pressed the seeds into the damp earth at the river's edge, where life and death blurred. He covered them carefully and left them there, trusting the ground to remember what to do.

I have to find the East Bear. Before...

Before what?

He didn't know. But the wand was pulling harder now. Insistent.

The boy ran.

The Great Tree appeared like a wall.

One moment: forest. Trees. Shadows.

Next moment: *this*.

The boy stopped so fast he nearly fell.

The tree was... he didn't have words.

It rose out of the forest like a world's spine – trunk wide as a street, crown lost in cloud, roots breaking the earth like the ribs of a buried giant.

And it was dying.

The boy could see it. The bark was grey in patches. Cracked. Weeping sap that looked like blood. Whole sections of the canopy were bare: skeletal fingers reaching for a sky they'd lost.

But parts were still alive, still green, still fighting.

Like the tortoise. Divided. Dying because it couldn't choose.

The boy approached it slowly.

At the base of the tree, between two massive roots, was an opening. A door. Or what used to be a door. Now it was just a gap in the bark, dark and uninviting.

The boy stepped through.

Inside was silence.

Not peaceful silence. The wrong kind. The silence of held breath. Of waiting.

The interior of the tree was hollow. A chamber shaped from living wood, its walls smooth and curved like ribs. Light filtered through cracks in the bark – thin, dusty shafts that barely reached the floor.

At the far end: a throne. Made of woven roots. Empty.

The boy's footsteps echoed.

"Hello?" His voice was too loud. Too small.

No answer.

He walked forward. Past the throne. Through another

opening into a second chamber.

This one was smaller. The walls were covered in carvings: scenes of the forest, of bears, of humans and animals living together. Tender. Intricate.

Old.

At the centre of the room: a pool of water. Clear. Still. Reflecting the light from above.

The boy knelt beside it. Looked into his own reflection.

For a second he saw himself: thin, scarred, marked by the ocean and everything he'd survived.

Then the reflection changed. The water clouded, filling with salt and motion. Waves. A leviathan grabbing a small sphere, smaller than a seed, before diving deep into the storm. The light in the water dimmed. A shadow crossed it, broad and unmistakable.

He turned.

A bear.

Dark-golden fur. Tired eyes. A scar across its muzzle.

The boy jerked back. The bear from the vision was here. Real. Solid. Standing in the doorway behind him.

It was huge.

Bigger than Snowy. Bigger than the old man. Easily twice the boy's height, its shoulders broad enough to fill the doorway completely.

Its fur was dark-golden, but dull. Matted. Stained with something even darker – blood, maybe, or ash.

It leaned on a staff. Oak. Carved with symbols the boy couldn't read. At its top: a crystal that pulsed with weak light.

The bear looked at the boy.

The boy looked at the bear.

For a long moment, neither moved.

Then the bear spoke. Its voice was deep. Raw. Exhausted.

"You shouldn't be here."

The boy's mouth was dry. "I'm looking for—"

"I know what you're looking for." The bear took a step forward. Limped. "The white bear. The one from the golden shore. The Fairy Queen must have sent you. I saw it in the waters."

"Yes. She—"

"Your bear isn't here," it said. "Not in these woods."

The staff scraped as the bear shifted its weight. A wince, swallowed.

"The golden shore – whatever door you came through – I can't reach it."

It glanced past the boy, listening to the walls as if they could betray him.

"And you can't stay. There's war in these roots. My brother sends things that don't tire."

The boy stared. The bear was covered in wounds. Cuts. Burns. Its fur was singed in places, frozen in others.

"You're hurt."

"I'm always hurt." The bear's eyes were impossibly tired. "That's what happens when you fight alone."

"Then why—"

"Because someone has to." The bear turned away. Its voice became soft and sad. "There's nothing here for you, child. Go home."

"I can't."

"Then go anywhere. Just not here."

The boy didn't move.

The bear stopped. Looked back over its shoulder.

"Why are you still here?"

The boy's hands clenched. "Because I came all this way. Because I faced the ocean and the shadow and the void.

Because the Fairy Queen said you could help me."

"The Queen was wrong."

"She said—"

"I don't care what she said." The bear's voice rose, sharp. "Look around you, child. The forest is dying. My brother from the West wants me dead. I'm fighting battles I can't win against enemies that keep coming. I have nothing to give you."

The boy took a step forward. "Then let me help you."

The bear laughed. It was a broken sound. "You? You're a child. What could you possibly—"

It stopped.

Its eyes went wide.

"Get down!"

The bear moved faster than anything that size should move. It shoved the boy aside, raised the staff.

And the wall exploded.

Something came through. Not through the door. Through the wall. Wood splintered. Light burst. The boy hit the ground hard, ears ringing.

He looked up. A creature stood in the ruined wall.

Taller than the bear. Much, much taller. Thicker. Wrong. Its body was grey and twisted, shaped like a man made from drowned limbs, with too many joints, too many bends, ending in claws that dripped something black. Where a face should be, there was only a wet mass of teeth and two black holes instead of eyes.

An octopus ogre, if such a thing could be named. A soldier of the West Bear.

The East Bear roared. Raised the staff. Light erupted from the crystal – white, blazing, sharp enough to make the boy's eyes water.

One beam hit the creature square in the chest – then the crystal *spat* a stray thread of light, scorching a carving near the ceiling. The bear tightened its grip, like it was holding a wound shut.

The creature screamed. Its body began to harden – grey turning to stone, stone sprouting green shoots, shoots becoming branches, each weaving bone and limb into the wall until the creature was no longer separate from it. The octopus-ogre was transforming. Becoming part of the Great Tree.

But it wasn't fast enough. Its fanged head and parts of its massive body were still free. Serpentine limbs lunged, snapping for the bear.

The bear swung the staff like a club. Connected. The creature's limbs flew backwards, crashed into the pool, shattered the water into a thousand silver drops.

The bear stumbled. Nearly fell.

The limbs were already rising.

And the bear was exhausted.

The boy saw it. The way the bear swayed. The way its grip on the staff trembled.

It's going to lose.

The boy grabbed the wand. Stood.

"Stay back!" the bear shouted.

The boy didn't listen.

He raised the wand. He didn't command. He tried to *feel* it: *Please stop it.*

The wand trembled. For a heartbeat, nothing answered. Then roots tore up through the floor – violent, splintering wood. They lashed out blindly, looping around the boy's ankle, the bear's foreleg, the creature's arm, hauling all of them short.

Pain flashed white. The bear snarled. He bit back a cry. *No – not like this. Not us.*

He held the feeling tighter, sharper: *Stop the beast.*

The roots shuddered. One by one, they loosened, slipping from the bear, falling from the boy before snapping back hard around the creature's limbs, pulling it towards the wall, holding it still.

The boy's arm went cold, as if the wand were drinking warmth out of him to pay for what it was doing.

The bear muttered, then raised the staff. One more beam. Clean. Final.

The creature became part of the tree. Fully. Its last scream cut off mid-cry, frozen in wood and leaf and stone.

From its open mouth burst a chorus of birds, small scurrying animals, and buzzing insects, flashing briefly in the light before scattering. When the final echo of sound dissolved, a strange, deep silence draped itself over the charred room, settling in a soft, comforting shroud.

The bear lowered the staff, its crystal still burning strong with fury. The bear's fury.

The East Bear sighed. Then it looked at the boy.

"You..."

That's when the boy stepped forward.

Smiling. Relieved.

Too close.

The bear's eyes went wide. "Don't!" the bear rasped, eyes fixed on the crystal. "It carries—"

Too late.

The staff's unconsumed fury hit, crystal glowing. The beam caught the boy mid-step, before the bear could pull it away.

Light – white, surgical.

Cold struck through his teeth.

His breath froze halfway out. He tried to blink and couldn't.

The wand petrified between knuckles that had been his hand.

Then—

Darkness.

The bear stared at the stone figure before it.

The boy. Frozen. Eyes wide. Mouth open. Reaching out. Trying to help.

"No." The word came out broken. "No, no, no..."

The bear dropped the staff. Fell to its knees.

"I didn't mean... You weren't supposed to..."

It reached out with one massive paw. Touched the boy's frozen face.

Stone. Cold. Unmoving.

The bear made a sound that wasn't a word.

It pressed its forehead to the boy's stone brow as if heat could be shared.

Once. Twice. Again – stubborn, useless.

"Foolish child!" the bear cried in anguish. "You stepped forward," it whispered. "You didn't even flinch."

Its breath fogged nothing. The stone stayed cold.

"You were trying to help," the bear whispered. "You were

just..."

The tree-room was silent except for the sound of the bear's breathing.

Heavy. Ragged.

Alone.

"I'm sorry," the bear said to the statue. "I'm so sorry."

It knelt there for a long time.

Then, slowly, it picked up the staff.

"Bravery shines brightest in the hearts of the lost... And deepens the shadows in the hearts of the living," the East Bear

sighed, looking at the frozen boy. "You tried to save what I couldn't," the bear said. "And I...

"I'll fix this," it finally said. Voice raw. Determined. "I don't know how. But I'll find a way. I promise."

The bear lifted the boy carefully – stone was heavy, but the bear was strong – and carried him out of the tree.

To the deep river where light still grew.

Where life still fought.

And there, surrounded by the last living roots of legendary trees, the bear began to sing.

Low. Steady. Mournful.

A song of healing. On the first low note, sap along the nearest tree loosened – dark, clotted, then clearer, beading like tears. On the second, a single green shoot pushed through ash at the waterline and held there, trembling.

A song the forest would remember.

Chapter VII: The Crystal Tree

«In shadowed woods, a boy's quest bright,
Seeks for the peace, united light
A battle fierce, an ogre's fall,
A stone-cast child, silence befalls.»

Profound silence reigned close to the river. The bear knelt on the ground close to the body. It stopped singing, shivering. Beside it, the magical staff lay discarded. Once a conduit of power, its brilliance was now extinguished.

The East Bear wrapped the boy in silk torn from its own cloak. Royal purple. The only beautiful thing it had left to give.

Then it laid him down.

Its massive paws trembled as they touched the frozen body. The boy's eyes stared at nothing. His mouth was open mid-word, reaching for something he'd never grasp.

The bear stayed there a long time. How long, it didn't know. Time felt wrong. Broken. Like something had stopped when the boy turned to stone, and forgotten how to start again.

Then, it dug.

The earth was soft. Rich. Alive. The bear's claws tore through roots and loam until a grave took shape – deep enough to hold a boy, wide enough for what needed to be done. Stone wasn't an end here – only a shell. The magical trees in this forest could take anything and make it part of themselves. But could they give life?

The East Bear lifted the body and gently placed him under the ground.

Before covering him, the bear reached into a pouch at its side and pulled out seeds. Small. Silver. Glowing faintly even in daylight.

Crystal Tree seeds. From the ancient tree that grew in the lake's depths, visible only on the darkest nights. The tree that sang melodies to summon both tears and smiles at once.

The tree that had been destroyed in the war with its brother.

These were all that remained.

The bear scattered them around the boy's body. Over his chest. Along his arms. In the earth beside his head.

"Grow," it whispered. "Please. Grow."

Then it began to cover him.

Layer by layer. Earth and leaves. Each handful a goodbye. Each moment a small death of its own.

When the grave was full, the bear sat back.

Stared at the mound.

And for the first time in decades, it wept.

The second night it came back.

Then the next. Then the next.

Seasons turned. He stopped counting them because counting hurt. Between fights and nights, each road a known track.

Each night, the bear sang.

There were no words at first. Not language. Just sound – low, mournful, threaded with magic as old as the forest itself.

The song was a prayer. A plea. A promise. Yet later, the words came.

"Come back. Please. Come back."

The forest listened. Trees leaned closer. The river slowed its rushing to hear. Even the wind stilled, holding its breath.

But the grave remained silent.

No shoots from it. No growth. Just earth.

The bear sang anyway.

Then, one morning, a sprout broke the soil where the boy's heart would be. Silver-white. Thin as thread.

The bear saw it at dawn and nearly collapsed with relief.

It had worked. *It was working.*

The sprout grew slowly – agonisingly slow. By the end of the month it was only as tall as the bear's smallest claw. Fragile. Easily crushed.

The bear built a barrier of stones around it. Stood guard. Sang louder.

Other sprouts followed. Six. Then twelve. Then twenty.

A forest of silver threads rising from the boy's grave.

Five years later, the bear started to lose hope.

The sprouts had grown into saplings – thin, delicate, beautiful. But they were just trees. There was no sign of the boy. No movement. No breath.

What if the spell wasn't enough? What if nothing was enough? What if he was truly lost?

The bear sat beside the growing grove and buried its face in its paws.

"I don't know if this is working," it said to the silent trees. "I don't know if you can hear me. I don't know if you're still in there or if you're... gone."

The trees swayed. The wind moved through their branches.

No answer.

The bear kept singing. Quieter now. More broken.

But it didn't stop.

It took a few more years for the saplings to become a tree. Not separate anymore. Intertwined. Woven together like fingers clasping. Their trunks had fused into one massive column – white, translucent, shimmering like frost under moonlight.

Leaves of delicate green trimmed with silver rustled with sounds like strings and chimes. The tree sang, even when the bear was silent.

And then: flowers.

Sienna-red. Glowing. Growing in clusters along the branches.

When they bloomed, the air filled with light.

When the petals fell, the flowers became fruits – crystalline, iridescent, pulsing with magic.

The bear buried each fruit at the tree's roots. Where they

touched earth, springs erupted – clear water threaded with light, feeding the tree, turning its white bark to soft glowing grey.

The bear's fur had gone pale. Its muzzle was grey. It moved slower now, its joints stiff.

But it sang.

Every night. Without fail.

Come back.

And when the twelfth summer came, it happened.

The bear sang for hours – melody woven with the same magic that he knew now by heart. Ancient magic, older than the forest, older even than the land beneath the forest.

It was then that the Crystal Tree shimmered. Its trunk glowed from within, pulsing in rhythm with the song as it lately had. Yet now, it was more rhythmic and its waves of light were stronger, rising from deep below.

A heartbeat.

The bear stopped singing.

Listened.

There. Again. Faint but real.

Thump.

Thump.

A soft whine escaped from its throat. Then it cried. Sang and cried. And danced and sang.

It was the boy's heart. Beating inside the tree.

Of that the bear was sure.

But then—

Inside the tree there was no light – no time, no body, no direction.

Only void.

And the worst part wasn't fear. It was *erosion.*

Memories thinning. Faces smearing at the edges. Names

slipping like wet ash. The boy felt like drowning. Yet this was different. Deeper.

Who was he?

A boy. He knew that. But what boy? What was his name?

Think. Remember.

But he couldn't. Voices faded. The golden beach, the polar bear, the fairies, the old man burning – all of it felt distant, drifting away. Dissolving.

No. No, I... I can't forget—

"Mum."

"Yes, sweetheart."

"I'm afraid of death," the boy said. And he was younger, much younger. Before—

"Of death?" Mother looked so beautiful that day. He could see her so clearly. She smiled. And her hands were warm, and smelt of cookies.

"Of forgetting. Losing who I was. Who I am." His voice broke. *"What if I lose the memory of all this? Of father... of you."*

Mum regarded him with her beautiful blue eyes. *"Memories are always part of this,"* she said, pressing a finger to his chest. *"Yet—"*

The boy held his breath.

Mum smiled. *"Look at that tree,"* she said, turning towards the orchard in their garden. *"When a tree dies, it feeds the forest."* She was serious, the way she was when reading a story. *"When a parent dies..."*

"He became silence," the boy said bitterly.

"Did he?" She flinched. *"No, dear. Your father became part of you. Who do you think your stubbornness belongs to? His. Your kindness. His. Your determination to keep going even when everything hurts.* His.*"*

Mum's voice was gentle but firm.

"Well..." She made that face when she was thinking. *"That stubbornness might be mine as well. You are everything that we are, and more. We're in every choice you make. Every word you speak. Every brave step you take."*

"But I wanted him. Not... not parts of him. I wanted him.*"*

"I know. But if you keep staring at what's gone, sweetheart, you'll miss the life still trying to reach you." She hugged him. *"Loss is real, my little one. But so is what comes after. You will grow stronger, and be a better man. Better than he ever dreamt."*

"And if I can't?"

"Then you'll stay a child forever, my honey pie." She tickled him, and they laughed.

Then the memory faded. He was back in the dark. Floating. And she was *gone.* But this time: *pain.*

Sharp. Real. Cutting through the void like a scream.

Something was piercing him.

He had a body again – he could feel it now, solid and trapped and wrong.

Roots.

They were inside him. Thin tendrils pushing through stoned skin, cracking the surface, burrowing deeper. The tree wasn't healing him the way humans healed. It was rebuilding him the only way it knew how – by turning him into itself first.

He tried to scream. *Couldn't.* His throat was wood.

The roots pushed further. Into muscle. Into bone. Wrapping around ribs. Threading through lungs that didn't breathe.

And then: *burning.*

Sap flooded his veins. Hot. Caustic. Liquid fire replacing blood.

His body convulsed – or tried to. The stone held him rigid.

But inside, everything was *burning, dissolving, reforming*.

The roots tightened. The sap hardened. His chest became bark. His fingers became twigs. His heart—

His heart stopped.

For one infinite second: *nothing*.

No breath. No pulse. No thought.

Just the void again. Numb. Welcoming him back.

This is it. This is where I stay.

And part of him – the tired part, the part that had fought so hard for so long – wanted to surrender.

It's easier here. No pain. No fear. No loss.

Just... nothing.

But then—

A sound.

Faint. Distant. But real.

Singing.

Deep and mournful and so full of longing it made something in the void explode. His heart moved just a beat. Then stopped again.

Someone was calling him back.

The bear.

The memory hit like lightning. The East Bear. The wall exploding. The creature. The light.

It petrified me.

By accident.

And now it's trying to bring me back.

The singing grew louder. Not in his ears. In his bones. In the wood that had replaced his flesh.

The bear was singing him alive.

I can go back. If I fight. If I try.

But it hurt. More than he could name.

The roots were still moving. The sap was still burning. His

body was being unmade and remade all at once and every second was agony.

I want to stop. I want it to end.

But the singing wouldn't let him.

Come back, it said. *Please. Come back.*

And beneath the song, another voice. Quieter. Older.

His mother's.

Not real. Just memory. But strong enough to matter.

Live, sweetheart. Even when it hurts. Especially when it hurts.

And his heart started to beat again. Stronger.

He reached towards the singing. Towards the pain. Towards life.

And the tree answered.

The roots that had been piercing him shifted. Became gentle. Cradling instead of crushing.

The sap that had been burning cooled. Became nourishment instead of poison.

The wood that had imprisoned him began to crack.

Small fissures at first. Then wider. Light seeping through – real light, golden and warm.

His lungs remembered how to breathe.

His heart remembered how to beat in rhythm.

His fingers – wood becoming flesh again – *twitched.*

The tree was letting him go.

No. Not letting. *Birthing.*

The bark peeled away. The roots uncurled. The wood split open like a flower opening to the light and—

Air.

Cold. Sharp. Real.

The boy gasped. Choked. His lungs seized, unused to breathing. He coughed – violent, wracking – and sap came up, dark yet fluid.

His eyes opened fully.

Blinding moonlight. *Too bright.* He squinted, tears streaming.

Shapes. Shadows. Movement.

And then: a face.

Massive. Furred. Golden-grey.

The bear.

It was crying.

The boy collapsed.

His legs... Did he have legs? The legs wouldn't hold him. He hit the ground, soft earth cushioning the fall.

Everything was too much. Too loud. Too bright. Too real.

His skin felt wrong. His body felt wrong. Like he'd borrowed it from someone else and it didn't quite fit.

He looked down at his hands.

They were *his*. Flesh. Warm. Trembling.

But different. Changed. He could feel it – something underneath the skin. Not quite wood anymore but not quite flesh either. Something in between.

"You..." he whispered. His voice was raw. Unused.

The bear knelt beside him. Wrapped him in something soft – a cloak, warm and heavy.

The boy frowned. Memories surfaced slowly, piece by piece.

Yes, he knew it. He saw... no, heard it. A golden bear. A vision. A battle. Light—

"You're the East Bear," he said. "You... you petrified me. I died," he said, wonder in his voice.

"Yes," the East Bear confirmed.

"I forgot everything. Became just... wood. And magic. And song."

"Yes."

"How long?"

"Twelve years."

The words hit like a blow.

Twelve years.

But his hands were still small. His body unchanged.

"Why don't I look older?"

"The tree held you outside time," the bear said quietly. "Your body didn't age. But the world did."

Twelve years.

Everyone he'd known – gone, changed, moved on. His uncle twelve years older. The other children adults now. The world a different place.

And him. Still a boy. But not really.

Something had been taken. Something he couldn't name.

Innocence, maybe. The belief that time was fair. That death could be reversed without cost.

"I'm cold," he said. Shivering. "Can you hold me?"

The bear embraced him. Its fur was warm. Solid. Real.

They sat like that for a long time. It felt good.

He fell asleep. And he *dreamed.*

He dreamt the way he sometimes did now – not the scattered, senseless dreams of ordinary sleep, but something sharper. The Crystal Tree that had birthed him still whispered truths meant for him alone.

Snowy was there, not far from the Crystal Tree. At the forest's edge. The East Bear was there too. Silent. No grey fur. Sitting beside the polar bear.

"You are troubled," the East Bear said to Snowy.

"I'm fine."

"You're a terrible liar. For a magical creature, anyway."

Snowy sighed. "He doesn't need me anymore. That's what's troubling me."

"The boy? Of course he needs you."

"Does he?" Snowy picked at its worn paw. "He has you now. You're wise. Powerful. Ancient. You can teach him things I never could. Show him things I never dreamt of. What am I compared to that? Just a toy. Just a... a leftover from childhood."

The East Bear was quiet for a long moment. "Do you know what I see when I look at you?"

"A shabby stuffed animal? Real only here?"

"I see a guardian who sat on a shelf for months, watching a child drown in grief, unable to do anything but wait. *Hoping*. Praying to forces older than names that one day, somehow, the door would open and you could help. That's what I see."

Snowy looked up, surprised.

"You love that boy," the East Bear continued. "Not with the love of age or wisdom or power. But with the love of presence. Of being there. Day after day, night after night, even when he forgot you existed. That's not a small thing, Snowy. That's perhaps the hardest thing of all."

"But I'm not... I'm not important like you are."

You are important, the boy wanted to scream. But felt his voice muted, as if beyond a screen.

"No," the East Bear agreed. "You're more important. Because he doesn't need ancient wisdom right now. He needs someone who knew his mother. Who sat beside him through the worst nights. Who chose to bring him through that door even knowing the risks." The eastern bear's eyes were kind. "He needs *you*. Not despite what you are, but because of it."

"You really think so?"

"I know so. I have wisdom, yes. Power, yes. But not all magic is loud and grand. I will never have what you have—"

But it didn't finish, as a sharp crack split the air – small, but wrong, like a branch snapping under no wind at all.

Snowy's ears twitched. The East Bear fell silent.

Another sound followed: the soft thud of sand shifting under hurried feet.

The boy felt it before he understood it – a pull, a tightening in his chest, as if something beyond the forest had just called his name without using a voice. And the dream shattered. And suddenly he was back – fully, sharply, painfully back – just as the wind changed and the waves of green roared louder than before. The forest shivered under a cold wind. His face felt cold.

"I came back." The boy looked up at the golden-grey bear. "I came back different. But I came back."

"You came back," the bear said. Its voice broke on the words. "Not untouched. But alive.

"Some things grew around you while you were gone," it added quietly. "Including grief."

Absence felt different now. Less like a wound and more like... *like a scar*. Still there. Still tender. But healed enough to touch.

Tears ran down his cheeks. They felt warm against the skin.

Eventually, the bear spoke.

"I'm sorry for the harm I caused you. In my eagerness to protect, I overlooked the strength found in patience and understanding."

The boy touched the bear's muzzle. Felt the wetness of tears there.

"It's not your fault. You were protecting yourself. I should have been more careful."

"No," the bear said firmly. "The fault was mine. But I've learnt. The tree taught me – growth requires patience. Even when you're strong. Especially if you're strong. Healing requires time. And some things cannot be rushed."

The boy looked at the Crystal Tree. It loomed above them, branches reaching for the sky, leaves singing softly in the wind.

"You grew this for me?"

"Yes."

"For twelve years?"

"Every day. Every night."

Tears pricked the boy's eyes. "Why?"

The bear's expression was impossible to read. "Because you tried to save me when I didn't deserve saving. Because you were brave when I was afraid. Because..." It paused. "Because you reminded me what I was fighting for."

The boy stood under the slowly rising sun. Unsteady. His legs remembered how to work, but barely.

He looked at his hands again. Flexed them.

Magic thrummed beneath his skin. Eager. Waiting.

He reached out – not with his hands, with his mind – and felt the forest respond.

A flower bloomed near his foot. Vines danced. The air shimmered.

"Whoa," he breathed.

The bear watched carefully. "The wand fused with you when the tree was born. You can shape the wood and all that is green with thought now. But—"

The boy wasn't listening. He was already experimenting. Making flowers bloom, vines twist, light dance between his fingers. It felt *incredible.* Like being alive and more than alive at once. When he tried a third flower, it opened wrong, pale at the edges. And the boy's vision swam for a moment as if the magic had taken a breath from him.

He wove threads of light and wood into clothing – shimmering, luminescent, beautiful.

"This is amazing!" he laughed.

The bear's expression darkened. "My boy. Listen to me."

The laughter died.

"The magic is yours. But it has limits. Use it frivolously and it will fade. Waste it and it will leave you. The tree gave you this gift, but nothing is free. Everything costs."

The boy's smile faltered. "What do you mean?"

"Magic is life force. Use too much, too fast, and you'll burn yourself out. Worse – use it selfishly, and it will corrupt. Become something twisted. Dangerous."

The boy looked at his hands. The power still thrummed there. But now it felt... *heavier*.

"How do I know if I'm using it right?"

"Intention matters. Healing, growing, nurturing – these strengthen the magic. Destroying for pleasure, taking for greed – these weaken it. And you." The bear's gaze was intense. "The wand was a tool you could set down. This magic is you now. You can't escape it. You have to live with it."

The boy swallowed.

The bear reached into its cloak and pulled out something wrapped in velvet.

"There is one more thing."

It unwrapped the cloth.

A seed. Small. Glowing softly with inner light.

"When the tree birthed you, this remained. It is... I don't know what it is. The heart of the spell, perhaps. Or the echo of your soul. Something essential."

The boy reached out. The moment his fingers touched the seed, warmth flooded through him.

This is me, he understood suddenly. *The song of me. The part that stayed alive while my body was stone.*

"What do I do with it?" he whispered.

The bear's eyes were sad. "That is for you to decide. But know this: it is precious. And fragile. Guard it carefully."

The boy cradled the seed against his chest. It pulsed in rhythm with his heartbeat.

They spent three days together.

The bear taught him to use the magic carefully – small things, deliberate things. Growing food. Healing wounds. Shaping wood.

"Never force," it said over and over. "Ask. Feel. Let the magic answer."

The boy practised. Failed. Tried again.

It was harder than he'd expected. The magic wanted to surge, to overwhelm, to do everything. Holding it back took effort.

"It will get easier," the bear assured him. "Or harder. Depending on what you feed it."

On the third night, the boy asked, "Do you know where my polar bear is? The one from the golden shore?"

The bear shook its head. "That path is not one I can walk. But the South Bear might know. It lives in the southern sea, where the darkness meets the sea."

"Can you tell me how to find it, please?"

The bear smiled. Tired but genuine. "I can tell you what I know." And it did.

When it finished, the bear embraced him one last time and gave him food and water for the road.

"You are braver than you know, little one. And kinder than the world sometimes deserves. Don't lose that."

The boy nodded, unable to speak past the lump in his throat.

He walked through the forest alone.

The trees watched him pass. The split between life and death was still there – but fainter now. Blurred at the edges.

At the midpoint, he stopped.

Pulled the seed from his pocket.

It glowed in his palm. Warm. Alive.

This is not for me to keep, he realised.

The bear had said the magic would fade if used selfishly. If hoarded.

This seed, this piece of himself, was meant to heal. Not to be kept.

He knelt.

Found a spot where the living forest met the dead one. Right on the border.

Dug a small hole with his hands.

And placed the seed inside.

The moment it touched earth, light erupted.

Not violent. Gentle. A wave of warmth that spread through the forest like a sigh.

The boy watched as the border dissolved. Dead trees sprouted green. Living trees reached towards their fallen brothers. The split began to heal.

Not instantly. Not completely.

But it started.

The boy stood. His chest felt lighter. Emptier.

He'd given up the seed. Given up the core of the magic that had been his.

Already, he could feel it – the power in his hands was fainter. Quieter.

But somehow, that felt *right.*

He reached the shore as evening fell.

The ocean waited. Vast.

The boy sat on the sand and stared at the horizon.

Twelve years, he thought. *Twelve years I was gone.*

He'd missed so much. Lost so much.

But he'd gained something too. Something he couldn't quite name.

Understanding, maybe. Or acceptance.

Death wasn't the end. But it wasn't nothing, either.

It cost.

And resurrection cost more.

He'd left a piece of himself in the forest. The seed. The core of his magic.

He'd never get it back.

Twelve years.

He tried to picture his uncle's face – older, sharper, maybe unrecognisable.

Tried to picture a world that had learnt to live without him.

His stomach clenched.

"I missed... everything," he whispered.

In that fleeting moment, the boy felt small against the immensity of the ocean, the green canopy of the forest, and the pale sky. A single note in a vast, unending song of growth, decay, and return.

And still, the song would be poorer without it.

He built a raft from the trees near the shore. His magic helped, but it was not easier. Each use burned like a flame inside his chest. Draining his breath.

When the raft was ready, he pushed it into the water, climbed aboard, and picked up the oar. And rowed towards the southern horizon, where the South Bear waited.

Behind him, the forest sang. A new melody, quieter than before. But whole.

The boy didn't look back.

Chapter VIII: The Sweet Delight

«Beneath the stars, where shadows play,
A bear and boy as night and day
Rebirthed they rose to tales of love,
In silence depth, they find their trove.»

The boy rowed south for three weeks.

On the fourth, the water changed.

Not all at once. Gradually. The blue darkened to grey, then black. The air grew thick. Heavy. Like breathing through wet cloth.

Fog rolled in, heavy, deliberate, wrong in its slowness: a gaping whale's maw made of clouds, swallowing the horizon piece by piece.

He stopped rowing. Listened.

Nothing. No birds. No waves slapping the raft. Just silence pressing against his ears.

The end of the world, he thought. His hands tightened on the oar. The wand-magic inside him stirred, uneasy.

He kept rowing anyway. Into the mist. The clouds slowly engulfed him.

Hours passed. Maybe days. Time felt broken in the fog.

Then the brume thinned into a different darkness – one that felt real, like pressure on the skin. Not fog-dark. Stone-dark.

The boy looked up. A dark sky, with tiny stars glinting through the haze. Or so he thought, until the mist slipped away. Rock arched above him, studded with diamonds. Not sky at all. Not a mouth either. More like a throat of stone, descending into the deep.

He made a torch out of wood and lit it. The flame revealed walls. A cavern. Enormous. The ceiling caught the light and threw it back.

The ocean had followed him beneath the world.

He extinguished the flame before it burned his hand. As he did, the torch fell onto the raft. The impact thudded through the wood, a sound that carried.

A hum. Faint. The echo from the depths changed. Warmer. Almost a mother's call in the dark.

The magic inside him leaned towards it.

He followed.

The cavern opened into a vast chamber.

And there, in the centre, rising from an island: *light*. Real light. Bright enough to hurt. A stone. Massive. Glowing like a star fallen into the earth.

The boy rowed towards it, his heart hammering.

As he got closer, the light revealed more. The island wasn't rock. The shore was brown. Soft. When he stepped onto it, his feet sank slightly.

He knelt. Scooped a handful. Not sand. Cocoa powder. Vanilla tingled in his nostrils, mingling with cinnamon's sharp sweetness and the earthy warmth of nutmeg. Each breath felt thick enough to taste.

The boy looked up.

Trees, not far from the shore, made of candy-canes. Rivers of cream. Mountains of crystallised sugar. Chocolate cliffs. Caramel waterfalls. Everything sweet. Everything edible.

His mouth watered. He didn't decide. He just... *started*.

A chocolate tree near the shore. He broke off a branch. It snapped clean. He bit into it.

Flavour exploded. Rich. Dark. Better than anything he'd ever tasted. For a moment the sweetness didn't just taste good

– it made the world quiet. It made him forget everything. A small, breathless laugh escaped him.

He ate the whole branch. Reached for another.

A cream river flowed past. He cupped his hands. Drank. Thick. Sweet. *Perfect.*

He found a lollipop tree. Bit into it. Shattered candy. He sucked the pieces, crunching them between his teeth.

Found caramel rocks. Soft. Chewy. He ate three. Six.

A gummy snake slithered past. He grabbed it. Bit its head off. It tasted like strawberries.

More.

He felt full but he didn't care. The hunger wasn't in his stomach. It was deeper. Insatiable.

I could eat this whole island, he thought.

And kept eating.

He didn't notice the bird at first. It was perched on a candy-cane tree, watching him. Small. Blue. Made of fudge. When he reached for the tree, the bird's feathers broke. Just... snapped off. Fell to the ground.

The boy paused. Stared at its wings.

The bird chirped. Not a happy sound. Pained.

He wiped his mouth. Chocolate smeared across his palm. Caramel under his nails.

He looked at the tree he'd just eaten. The trunk was oozing. Clear liquid seeping from the bite marks.

The sweetness turned thick in his throat.

It's fine. It's just... candy. It'll grow back. He kept eating. But he saw it now. Every bite left damage.

The cream river he'd drunk from... it was flooding now, rising from the place his touch had wounded it. The caramel rocks he'd eaten – the cliff they'd come from was giving way, shearing off in slabs that plunged into the rising cream. The gummy snake he'd killed... the others were fleeing, their colours leaching out as they moved, as if something unseen were draining them.

The boy's chest tightened.

I should stop. But he didn't.

He found a chocolate flower. Bit off its petals. They tasted like honey. The stem withered. Turned grey. Fell.

His mouth filled; his hands kept moving.

He ate a candy-cane sapling. Crunched it between his teeth. Each bite popped and fizzed on his tongue, a rush bright enough to drown everything else. The tree beside it shuddered. Its hard, sweet leaves fell, shattering when they hit the ground.

A thought surfaced – clear, small: *Enough.*

Yet his hands reached for a caramel bird's nest. Pulled out eggs. Crushed them in his fist. Licked the caramel from his fingers.

The mother bird – chocolate, wings spread – dove at him. He swatted it away. It hit the ground. One wing bent wrong. It couldn't fly.

The boy stared at it.

It was chirping. High. Desperate.

What am I doing. His hand was already moving towards the next thing.

He didn't stop until he physically couldn't eat. His stomach hurt. His throat was raw. His hands were shaking. He collapsed against a cheese-wall – white chocolate and cream cheese pressed into bricks. And he ate some. Because of course he did. The chocolate ran down his chin like joy pretending to be real.

Rest now, his mind murmured. And he surrendered to sleep – a dark, dreamless sleep.

As he drifted, a curious creature alighted nearby: a bird cloaked in blue fudge. It paused to study him with unsettling interest. Its eyes, dark and uncannily human, seemed to look straight through him, past flesh, past time.

With a soft chirp, as if mourning some truth he couldn't yet know, it shook its head. Then, with a touch that felt like both warning and mercy, it grazed his cheek with its claws before vanishing into the mist.

Upon awakening, the boy breathed hard. Looked back at the path he'd taken.

Oh.

Oh no.

The island was destroyed. Puddles of melted chocolate everywhere. Cream rivers overflowed, drowning sugar-trees. Dead creatures scattered across the ground – gummy, caramel, chocolate. Some half-eaten, others crushed. Some just... gone.

The colours were wrong. Dull. Grey spreading like infection.

The boy's vision blurred. His eyes burned. He refused the relief of crying.

I didn't mean...

But he had. He'd seen the damage. He'd kept going anyway. His stomach lurched. He turned and vomited. Chocolate and caramel and cream, bitter now, burning his throat.

When he finished, he was shaking.

What have I done?

Two hands grabbed him. Rough. Hard. He yelped, too weak to fight.

Soldiers. Two of them. Made of crystallised sugar – translucent, sharp-edged, their armour clicking with every movement.

They slammed him face-down against the cheese-wall. One pressed a sword to his neck. Sugar-glass. Sharp enough to cut.

The boy froze.

The soldiers spoke. Not with mouths – they had only chiselled mouths. The sound came from inside them. Like wind through crystal.

And they spoke in turns, finishing each other's sentences:

"You're fortunate..."

"...that you bear the mark."

"Otherwise..."

"...you'd be dead."

The boy's mind raced. "Mark? What mark?"

One soldier pointed to his cheek. Where the blue fudge bird had scratched him, back when he was sleeping.

"The one-crisp-bird..."

"...marks only kings..."

"...or those the King allows to live long enough to kneel."

"Clearly..."

"...you're not royal."

"Of that much..."

"...we're certain."

"But you..."

"...are protected."

They hauled him to his feet. The sword stayed at his throat.

"You destroyed..."

"...the joy-palace."

"Severe punishment..."

"...is warranted."

"Rebuild the wall..."

"...and you shall face our true King."

The boy's throat was dry. "That's what I want. To see the King."

The soldiers didn't respond. Just positioned themselves on either side of the hole he'd eaten through the cheese-wall.

Guarding him.

The boy looked at the wall. And began to work.

Rebuilding was harder than destroying.

Destroying had been easy. Thoughtless. Fun.

This was exhausting.

The cheese bricks were heavy. Each one had to be cut from the cliff nearby, shaped, fit into place with cream mortar.

His hands blistered. His back ached. Sweat dripped into his eyes.

And with every brick, he saw more damage around.

The chocolate birds with broken wings. The caramel creatures trapped in hardening cream. The sugar-trees bleeding red syrup from their wounds.

I did this.

Not on purpose. But that didn't matter.

The boy set down the brick he was holding.

"I have to fix it," he said aloud.

The soldiers didn't respond.

The boy left the half-built wall and set himself towards harder work. Using magic, brute force – anything that would hold.

He worked until his arms stopped feeling like his own: redirecting cream back into its beds, prying gummy bodies from hardening syrup, setting broken blossoms upright with shaking hands. Some things hadn't survived his hands. He learnt to leave them. That hurt worse than the blisters.

He cleaned the springs. Replanted crushed flowers. They steadied under his care, colour stirring back into them. He set one broken chocolate bird upright and it fell again, head first, as if the island couldn't trust him yet.

Each act of repair made him feel slightly less sick. But only slightly.

When the island looked... not whole, but liveable again... he collapsed.

His body hurt everywhere. A hot thread slid from his nostril. He wiped it; his fingers came away red.

His magic felt thin. Each use during the repair had cost him. He could feel it – a hollowness in his chest where the wand-magic used to thrum.

But the island was breathing again.

The boy dragged himself back to the wall.

And finished it.

Brick by brick. Slow. Aching.

When the final brick was in place, he sat back. Stared at his hands. Blistered. Covered in cream mortar and chocolate dust. Shaking.

He did not feel forgiven. But he felt awake.

The soldiers led him through the palace.

Massive doors. Mosaic of hard-candy jewels. One soldier knocked. Disappeared inside.

An aged sweet-cheese scent escaped through the opened doors as the soldier returned.

"The King..."

"...will see you."

"Enter..."

"...alone."

The boy stepped through.

The throne room wasn't what he expected. It felt... undecided, like a stage without an audience.

No throne or court. Just a bear. Small. Covered in dark velvet fur dusted with sugar crystals. Chocolate drops on its paws. A tiny gold-chocolate crown perched on its head.

And it was moving. Constantly. Restless.

The South Bear was at a table, working.

The boy watched.

The bear scooped cocoa powder in its paws. Breathed on it. The powder... moved. Shaped itself. Became a balloon animal made of chocolate.

The bear breathed again. The chocolate creature shivered. Took a breath of its own. It ran across the floor and disappeared down a tunnel.

So, this is how the island was created, reflected the boy.

"Indeed." The bear didn't look up. *It had heard him think.* Its voice was warm. Amused. It kept working, shaping more creatures without looking at him. "What you seek isn't here."

The boy's stomach dropped.

"At least, not yet." The bear turned. Looked at him with eyes that were impossibly deep.

You came for your polar bear. But that's not why you're really here. The thought brushed his mind before he even knew it was there. The boy flinched. The bear hadn't spoken aloud.

Yet it was right. This thought registered late.

"I..." He didn't know how to say it. "I came because I don't know who I am anymore."

Go on. The same thoughts whispering in his mind. Not his thoughts.

"I died. Or... I think I died. I was stone. Then I was wood. Then I was... reborn. But I'm not the same. I don't feel the same." His hands clenched. "And then I came here and I... I destroyed everything. I saw what I was doing and I kept doing it anyway. Why? Why did I do that?"

The bear blew on another handful of cocoa. A chocolate bird took shape. Flew away.

Why do you think?

"I don't know."

Yes, you do.

The boy's throat tightened. "Because I wanted to. Because it felt good. Because I could."

And?

"And I didn't care what it cost."

The bear nodded. Set down the cocoa. Looked at him directly.

"Joy unbalanced is greed," it said simply. "This kingdom is

woven from my breath. To take without care is to seize not the sweetness alone, but the song that binds it into being."

The boy shivered. That was exactly what he'd done. He dropped to his knees. "I'm so sorry. I destroyed—"

"Stop."

The bear's voice was soft. Not angry. Almost gentle.

The boy looked up. The South Bear sat heavily, its velvet coat dusted with cocoa, its paws stained with chocolate. It looked tired in a way he hadn't expected.

"This realm was flawless in form, yet empty," the bear said, the word bitter. It gestured towards where the repaired wall, the cleaned springs, the restored trees would be. "I shaped wonders, for such is my charge. Yet none dared to enjoy them, and so they lay hollow."

The boy's throat tightened. "But I—"

"You shattered my wall, muddied my springs, broke my branches, and yes – you took life. These wounds are real, and they will live in you. Yet you loved this realm in the way it was fashioned to be lived in." Something cracked in its voice.

"My father told me: *'Bring delight without turning it to pain.'* I thought that meant protecting everything. But he meant: create generously, and let go gracefully."

From the crown of the palace, it looked out over the kingdom through an aperture: the imperfect wall, the sweetened springs, the leaning trees.

"When you devoured that first branch, laughing without restraint, it was the first true joy this kingdom had heard in centuries," the bear murmured. *I tried to keep everything perfect... but perfection is a lonely kingdom. Things must be touched, changed, even broken, or they never truly live.*

"I destroyed everything," the boy whispered.

"And then you rebuilt it. Not just the wall I bade you mend, but the countless things your joy had broken. Not in full – but enough for the realm to breathe again."

The bear rose and touched his shoulder.

"So... you're not angry?"

"Angry?" The bear laughed, warm as melting chocolate. *How could a king of joy hold anger? You reminded me what this place is for. To be ruined by love.*

From its coat, the South Bear drew a crystallised drop of honey, clear as glass. "This was my father's final bequest – a moment of pure sweetness." It glowed ever so softly. "I guarded it through ages, fearing the loss of what I treasured."

It held it for a moment in its paws, eyes glimmering.

"Take it," the bear finally said. "Use it. Break it open. Let it be what it was meant to be."

The honey warmed in the boy's palm.

"When you leave," the bear said, "remember: the things you love will change." *They'll break. They'll be consumed by time and use and joy.* "That isn't tragedy. That's life."

The boy's eyes burned. He looked at the floor.

"You are one who errs, and one who mends," the bear said. "That is the measure of a worthy heart."

A soft warmth settled in the bear's gaze, as if weighing the boy's spirit and finding it ready.

"You have learnt what you came here to learn," it murmured. "Now your path turns to wisdom beyond ice." *Legend holds that my eldest brother knows trails unknown to any living soul, and it alone may guide you towards your polar bear.*

The South Bear's gaze deepened, as though seeing the road already unfolding before the boy. "Few seek the North Bear," it said. "Fewer still are ready."

The boy wiped his eyes. "But how do I find the North Bear? Do you know where it is?"

The bear smiled. *Follow the needle-current – you'll feel it in your bones, even through the fog. When you see a claw-shaped star, turn towards it. Towards the place where sun and moon meet and snow never melts.*

The bear swept its paw across the table. The cocoa powder shifted, forming continents, oceans, mountains. A map drawn in chocolate.

"Behold." The bear pointed on the chocolate-map to where the North Kingdom lay.

Go forth, not burdened by the stones of yester deeds, but with a heart attuned to compassion.

"Thank you."

"Return when your spirit calls you back," the bear said. *My den stands open to you always – for guidance, for comfort, or simply for the joy of friendship.*

The boy's throat was too tight for words. He rose, steadied himself, and bowed. "Until our paths cross again... farewell, South Bear," he managed.

They shall, the bear thought with quiet certainty once the boy had turned away.

Outside, on the chocolate shores, the boy set to work. He shaped a smaller, swifter raft, chipping the aged wood with careful hands and fitting the remaining cores into place. Piece by piece, a nimble vessel took form – light, pliant, ready to answer his will. His hands worked automatically. The magic helped – weak now, but still there.

When the boat was ready, he pushed it into the water.

Climbed aboard.

Looked back at the island one more time.

The star still glowed. The island still lived.

But the boy knew: he'd left scars there. Invisible ones. In the creatures he couldn't save. In the trees that would never grow back quite right.

He closed his fingers around the honey drop.

Its warmth pulsed faintly, as if reminding him of what the South Bear had said – that sweetness hoarded turns hollow, and beauty untouched becomes a kind of sorrow.

He held it to his chest, feeling the weight of what he'd broken... and what he'd begun to understand.

Then picked up the oar.

And rowed.

Through darkness and fog, until the ocean met the sky and salt stung his lips once more.

Northward he sailed, towards the realm of ice and wisdom, where the eldest of all bears kept counsel with the cold.

Chapter IX: The Four Griffins

«In realms of sweets, where dreams unfold,
Through shadowed cave, arcane of old,
A boy learns truth beneath the light,
Compassion's depths in chocolate's might.»

The boy rowed for a day, the boat rocking above the long northern current pulling at it. At night he wrapped himself in layers of wood, like a stem sealed inside a seed. And he slept, dreaming of endless forests, of waterfalls, of cliffs rising and falling in whispers of green.

But on the second day, hunger found him.

He reached into his pocket and felt the honey drop – clear as glass, warm as a heartbeat.

He touched it to his tongue.

Sweetness bloomed.

The sea shivered. The horizon folded like silk drawn through a ring. Wind curled around him in a slow, deliberate spiral, as if remembering a pattern it had once known and misplaced.

He rowed.

Each stroke felt ordinary – the wood's creak, the waves' spray, the sweat stinging his skin. But the sea did not answer with distance. His boat slid forward in great, quiet strides with a steadiness that wasn't the tide. Sunrise came. Then came again before the salt on his forearms had dried.

When sleep took him, it was instant – a blink – and behind his eyes there was only dark. Not even a whisper of green. As though something had been taken from him.

On the next morning, he tasted the honey again. The

sweetness hooked behind his ribs, and the sea answered like a trained thing: waves flattened into lanes, and the fog peeled apart into a narrow, bright corridor the raft could not miss.

He rowed through it as though the world had been gently folded to meet him halfway. He felt no hunger, no thirst, no fatigue. Just an absence, clean and cold.

And when he collapsed tired under the cover of wood, there was no rest. Sleep cut out, and he woke with the taste of nothing in his mouth. The daylight felt desaturated, distant.

By the next day, the crystallised honey had thinned to a sliver. He held it in his palm, watching it glow. His hand looked wrong. Too still. As if it belonged to someone else. Salt had dried into a second skin. His lips were split.

He tasted the last of the honey.

And the world didn't bend this time – it let go of him, and he drifted forward like a thing being carried. Sunrise, sunset, sunrise, every one too fast to count. The stranger he had become rowed. The world turned thin and unreal, as if the sea were a picture sliding beneath him. But nothing was left for his sleep. He sat beneath his wooden layers, aware of the dark. Of silence. Of everything.

Morning hit like a slap.

Cold bit through his wooden layers and into bone. His tongue felt thick. His throat closed around a dry swallow.

Hunger arrived. Not a thought. A claw. He tore into his reserves, eating until the shaking eased.

The sea sounded loud again. Real again. The water turned black. Ice appeared in chunks, floating past like splintered bone. He rowed, feeling each wave like a slap against muscles drawn tight. The sun inched above him.

When the night finally came, he shivered, and shivered. Pulled layers over layers, until sleep found him.

Nightmares. A cry of his mother. A plea from his father. Something *burning*. And him, moving slowly towards a closing door.

He woke up covered by a thin layer of frost. Each exhale crystallised into glimmers that vanished like whispered secrets.

The North had found him.

Far ahead, rising from the mist – crushed ice. A wall of it above the ocean, white and endless.

The boy stepped onto the shore. His feet sank into snow up to his knees. Cold bit through his clothes immediately.

An ocean of white, he thought, looking up. He felt small again, like a letter of ink on a blank page.

In the distance, barely visible through falling, spiralling snow: a palace. Carved from the glacier itself. Spires reaching towards a grey sky.

The boy reshaped his raft into a sleigh – sealed, insulated, barely holding heat. His magic responded sluggishly. The cold made everything harder.

One day later, after slopes that tried to throw him and crevasses that opened like mouths, the palace rose out of the storm.

He was exhausted. And freezing. His fingers were numb. His face hurt. Even breathing felt like swallowing glass.

But there it was: the entrance. Immense doors of metal and ice, bearing symbols he couldn't read.

And in front of the doors, four towers anchored this northern citadel.

On each tower: a griffin.

White. Enormous. Wings folded. Watching.

The boy climbed off his sleigh. His legs shook.

One griffin lifted its head. Looked directly at him.

Then dropped from its tower.

It didn't fall. It *descended* – wings spread, graceful despite its size. Silent as snowfall. Beyond it, the other three did not move; yet the boy felt their attention upon him, unyielding.

The griffin landed ten feet in front of him.

The boy's shadow disappeared beneath the griffin's.

He'd thought the East Bear was big.

This was different.

The griffin was *tall.* Towering. Its head level with the palace's second story. Its wings, even folded, were wider than the boy's height.

White feathers. Gold eyes. Beak sharp enough to split

stone.

The boy couldn't move.

Not fear. Weight. The griffin's presence pressed against him like weather. Locked within the griffin's gaze, he felt small. Measured.

The griffin spoke.

Not in a language. In *languages* – layered, overlapping, some human, some utterly alien. The boy's ears couldn't separate them. Then, cutting through: one clear voice.

"*Welcome, traveller.*"

The boy's mouth was dry. "H-hello," he managed.

The griffin's head tilted. Studying him. The boy shifted slightly, an instinctive reaction; yet he did not look away. *Had it ever seen a human?*

"What bringeth thee unto the North, child of warmer londes?"[26] intoned the griffin, frowning.

The boy swallowed. Found his voice. "I seek the North Bear. The wise one. I need... guidance."

"Many seek our King," the griffin said. Its voice was impossibly deep. "Few are worthy."

"I'll do whatever it takes."

The griffin's eyes narrowed. Not angry. Measuring.

"Then hear this: four trials await thee. Pass them, and thou may stand before Its Majesty. Fail, and the North shall claim thee."[27]

The boy's chest tightened. "What kind of trials?"

"The first beginneth now."[28]

The griffin spread one wing and drew from between its

---

[26] What brings you here in the North, child of warmer lands?
[27] Then hear this: Four trials await you. Pass them, and you may stay before Its Majesty. Fail, and the North shall claim you
[28] The first [trial] begins now.

feathers a golden bowl, setting it gently on the snow between them.

"Fill this," the griffin said, "with the roe of cold-water salmon. Not the flesh. The future bound within it. Not taken by force. Not stolen. Earned."

The boy stared at the bowl. "Where do I find—"

"That is thy task to discover." The griffin's wings unfurled fully, casting the boy in shadow. "Thou hast until the moon's next eclipse. Three days. Fail, and thou shalt not proceed."[29]

Wind kicked up. Snow swirled.

When it cleared, the griffin was gone.

The boy was alone with an empty bowl and a riddle he didn't understand.

He picked up the bowl. Gold. Heavy. Beautifully made.

Salmon roe. Cold-water salmon.

The boy looked around. Ice. Snow. Mountains. No rivers. No lakes visible.

Not taken by force. Not stolen. Earned.

What did that mean?

He stood there, shivering, trying to think.

Then realised: *I'm freezing.*

He needed shelter. Warmth. Time to figure this out.

The boy climbed back into his sleigh and pedalled away from the palace, searching for anything out of the wind.

The land dipped. Deep. Sheltered from the worst of the gale. Still freezing.

He slowed without meaning to.

Something in the ice felt familiar. Heavy.

He followed it down into the valley.

---

[29] That's your task to discover. [...] You have until the moon's next eclipse. Three days. Fail, and you shall not proceed.

The boy tried to make fire. It sparked. Died. Sparked again. Finally caught. He huddled close to the warmth, trying to think.

Salmon. Cold-water salmon.

Where would salmon be in a place like this?

Rivers? But everything's frozen.

Unless...

The boy looked down. At the ice beneath him.

Felt its micro-tremors. A dull ache spread in his hands as he rested them on the ice.

Where a valley should be, water would have nowhere to go. It would press. It would push. Making the ground tremble.

Rivers trapped beneath. Frozen over but still flowing.

That's where the salmon would be.

He felt a surge of hope.

The boy fashioned his sleigh into a drill moulded around his body: crude, improvised, powered by magic and mechanical force. It took hours. By the time he finished, his hands were bleeding. His magic felt thin. Stretched. But the drill worked.

He positioned it over where the ground dipped, where the pressure felt wrong, and began to drill.

The drill screamed, his own muscles amplified by wheels and levers. Ice chips flew. Down. Down. Down. Thirty feet. Fifty. A hundred.

The boy's muscles burned. The magic holding the wood together flickered.

Keep going.

At two hundred feet, the drill broke through into a narrow cave and dropped hard, tearing through the ground beneath him.

Water surged up – freezing, fast-moving. Faint blue-green

threads stirred in the current. They brightened where the river strained against stone and crystal veins. The crystals flashed in brief answer.

The boy scrambled back as the water rushed past his boots, biting cold, relentless. For a heartbeat, silver shadows flickered deep through the glow – long, swift. Then the current snapped empty.

A river.

He had found it.

The stream seized the broken ice and tore it away, roaring through the cave hard enough to shake the walls. The drill lay half-submerged, wheels spinning uselessly as water poured past. The boy pressed himself to the stone, breath ragged, fingers numb as cold gnawed through his wood-threaded gloves.

The river did not care that he had found it. It rushed on, ancient, carving its path through the dark. He watched it, chest heaving, until the tremor in his legs eased.

Then he looked at the golden bowl strapped to his sleigh.

Salmon would come here. They had to. But whatever had flashed beneath the surface was gone.

The boy dragged himself onto the frozen ground, away from the pull of the water. He kindled another fire and dried his clothes. Warmed his hands. His chest. Then he returned to the flow beneath the ice. It moved fast. He couldn't see the bottom.

How do I catch them?

He fashioned a net from the broken pieces of his drill and lowered it into the current.

He waited until his arms shook, then hauled it up.

Empty. Only ice-foam and torn weed.

He tried again, harder, and got the same answer.

By the time the thin light above began to fade, his shoulders were knotted with failure, and the river hadn't offered him a single flash of life.

That dusk, when the sun dipped below horizon, huddled close to the fire, the boy tried a different thought.

Not taken by force. Maybe that was the problem. He had been trying to *take* them. *Earned.* How do you *earn* fish?

He thought of the South Bear's lesson. Of consumption and care. Of balance.

Maybe I need to give them something first. But what did salmon want? Food?

He searched his supplies. There was nothing a salmon would eat. Unless...

He looked at his hands. At the cuts left by the drill.

Blood.

No. That's insane.

But the thought wouldn't leave him.

Blood calls to blood. Life calls to life.

The boy drew a slow breath. He pressed his fingers together and let three drops fall into the river below.

Nothing happened.

He wrapped his hand. Felt stupid. Sat there longer than he meant to.

Blood was still *taking*.

The river said nothing.

He tried to sleep. Couldn't. His mind raced.

Three days... I'm failing. I can't even pass the first trial.

What made me think I was ready for this?

The griffin's words returned to him, heavy as stone. *Few are worthy.*

Maybe I'm not. The thought settled in his chest and would not move.

The next day, desperate, the boy tried everything.

The more he forced the water – roots probing, nets snapping open – the quieter it became, until even the sound of the current felt like distance.

Nothing worked.

By evening, he'd caught exactly zero salmon.

Two days until the eclipse.

The boy sat by the river, staring into the shimmering waves.

I don't know what to do.

For the first time since leaving the South Bear, he felt truly lost. Not in body. In spirit.

I thought I was ready.

Maybe some things could not be rushed. He wasn't wise enough. He looked down at his bleeding hands. *That much was certain.*

His gaze drifted to the drill he had forced through the ice. To the nets that had caught nothing.

I tried to take by force, he realised. *Again. Instead of understanding.*

On the third day, the boy didn't try to fish.

He just sat by the river. Watching the water move below. Listening. Thinking.

Not taken. Earned.

What does the salmon need? What can I offer?

He had no answer. The eclipse would end before he was ready. He'd failed.

The boy lifted the golden bowl and stared into it.

Empty. Only his reflection.

He'd come so far. Faced the ocean. The leviathan. Death itself. Resurrection.

And now he would fail.

Because he could not catch fish.

As evening drew near, he made his way back to the ice palace. Slowly. Dreading each step.

The griffin waited, perched atop its tower. When it saw him approach, it descended. Landed. Its gaze moved over the boy's scars. Then to the bowl in his hands.

Empty.

"Thou hast failed,"[30] the griffin said. There was no anger in its voice. Only fact.

"I tried. I couldn't... I don't know how to—"

"The trial was not to catch fish," the griffin said. "It was to learn what it truly meaneth to earn."[31]

The boy looked up.

The griffin's eyes were sad. "Many seek to take. Few learn how to receive."

"I don't understand."

"No," the griffin said. "But thou mayest yet."[32]

It spread its wings.

"Return with the bowl filled before the next moon withheld, or return not at all. The choice is thine. The North turneth away no willing seeker – only those who mistake force for worth."[33]

Wind swirled. The griffin rose.

The boy was alone again.

He stood there a long time, staring at the empty bowl.

I failed.

---

[30] You have failed.

[31] [...] It was to learn what it truly means to earn.

[32] No. [...] But you may yet.

[33] Return with the bowl filled before the next moon eclipse, or do not return at all. The choice is yours. The North rejects no willing seeker – only those who think strength is the same as worth.

The words sat heavy. But beneath them, something else stirred.

The trial wasn't to catch fish. It was to understand.

He looked at his bleeding hands. His scars. The desperation beneath them.

I tried to force it. Just like I forced my way through everything else. The leviathan. The East Bear's heart. Even the chocolate island. He had taken and taken until...

The boy sat down in the snow and closed his eyes.

What did it mean to earn, rather than take?

Under the ice, something moved. A shimmer, older than memory.

He still did not have the answer.

Chapter X: The Drops of Water

«Four Griffins guard the northern snow,
Testing the hearts that dared to go.
The empty bowl, the river deep,
Showed him what force could never keep.»

Frost and snow hid everything that mattered. The boy drew a breath that burned his throat and told himself, "I'll do whatever it takes to find my way home."

The wind took the words and left nothing behind.

He pushed himself upright, looked once more at the four griffins, then turned back to the valley. Back to the cave. Back to the river.

And there, he sat.

For two days he didn't fish. Didn't solve. He watched the black water run under ice and let the fire's weak glow do what it could.

On the third day, something shifted. Not outside. Inside.

The boy was tired. Hungrier than he had been in weeks. But his mind was clearer.

I can't force this, he thought, watching the rush of waters below. *I can't trick it or outsmart it or conquer it.*

So what can I do?

He thought of the Crystal Tree. Of how the East Bear had spent twelve years singing to it. Not forcing. Not demanding.

Just tending. Patiently. With love.

That was what earning meant.

The boy looked at his hands. At the cuts from the drill, still healing.

Blood.

He had let a few drops fall into the river before, driven by desperation.

But what if that instinct had not been wrong? What if it had simply been incomplete? The thought would not leave him.

Life calls to life.

This is insane. Blood doesn't summon fish.

The boy drew a steady breath. He lowered his hand into the river until the cold found the half-healed cuts the drill had left behind.

The skin opened again – small, clean lines – and a thin red thread drifted into the current.

More than before. Enough that his head spun and his pulse thudded in his ears. He wrapped his hand tight before the noise could become panic.

Then he sat back.

Waited.

Nothing happened for an hour.

Then something answered.

Not a fish.

A tremor at the river's lip, where the blood had touched. A thin, red sprout pushing through frozen earth.

The boy's breath caught.

It grew faster. Stem thickening. Branches spreading.

A tree.

Its bark was dark red. Its leaves crystalline. Like frozen rubies.

Blood Tree, he thought – because nothing else fit.

It was growing from his blood. Fed by the river. Thriving in impossible conditions.

Within an hour, it was as tall as the boy. Within two, it towered.

Its roots spread through the riverbed. Its branches reached

up towards the hole in the ice, towards light. And on those branches: fruit, red, glowing faintly.

The boy stared.

Then he climbed down to the river's edge and touched the trunk.

Warmth pulsed beneath the bark – steady, intimate – as if the river had learnt his name and was speaking it back through wood.

You're alive, the boy thought. *Really alive.*

The tree's branches swayed, though there was no wind.

The boy picked one of the fruits. It came away easily, warm in his palm. He bit into it.

Sweetness burst, rich, with an aftertaste like iron. And something else.

Memory.

His mother's voice, sudden and close. His father's laugh, warm against his ear. Sun on sand. Waves between his toes.

The fruit held pieces of him.

Because it came from me.

The boy ate two more fruits. Saved the rest. Then realised: the fruit's scent was drifting. Through the cave. Into the river. And the salmon were coming.

He could see them now – silver shapes moving through dark water, drawn by the smell.

They want the fruit. The boy's heart raced. *This is it. This is how I earn them.* But he couldn't just grab them. That was taking. He needed to offer.

He worked through one aching day.

He wove a net from the Blood Tree's shed twigs – springy, strong – then shaped it into a wide enclosure with gaps that could be drawn closed.

At dusk he crushed one fruit into pulp and let the current carry its scent like a question.

The salmon came.

Slowly at first. Then in numbers.

They circled the enclosure. Curious. Hungry.

The boy watched, heart pounding.

Come on. Please.

One salmon entered. Then another. Then ten.

The boy waited until twenty were inside. Then gently, so gently, closed the gaps. The salmon were trapped. But not harmed. The netting was soft. The space large enough for them to swim.

I'm sorry, the boy thought to them. *I won't hurt you. I promise.*

He didn't take anything that day. Nor in the following week. He fed them instead, guiding fresh water through the enclosure and keeping them healthy and well fed.

But the cave was starving: the fire ate his wood, the cold ate the rest, and the Blood Tree needed light that flame couldn't give.

He expanded the cave. Built up steps into the walls. From the ice he carved, the boy cut clear blocks and set them together into a pyramid above the entrance. The structure sealed the tunnel to the surface. Its angles caught what little daylight and aurora reached this depth and bent it downward, gathering it into a single, steady beam.

The light fell upon the Blood Tree, and the tree grew.

What the pyramid did not gather, it scattered. Colour drifted across stone and root, warming wood and flesh alike.

On the tenth day – when the moon's light thinned and vanished – the salmon turned, circled, and began to lay roe.

The boy had been waiting for this. He harvested carefully. Reverently. Taking only what the bowl required, leaving the rest to the river. Each egg went into the golden bowl with a whispered: *Thank you.*

When the bowl was full, he opened the enclosure.

Expected the salmon to flee.

They didn't scatter.

A few held close to the net as if waiting for him. As if reluctant to leave. They brushed his hands tenderly.

You trust me, the boy realised, eyes burning.

He watched them finally swim away, back into the dark river.

"Under the freezing waves, where shadow holds, I see no hunter, nor the hunted be. Just souls," he whispered. *Go,* he thought. *Be well. Maybe we'll meet again.*

The boy climbed out of the valley.

The Blood Tree stayed behind, growing strong beside the

underground river.

He would return to it. He knew that. It was part of him now.

But first: the griffin.

He reached the palace as dawn broke.

A griffin descended. Not the first one. This one's feathers had blue tints at the edges.

The second griffin.

It looked at the bowl in the boy's hands.

Full. Glowing faintly with the salmon roe's life.

"Thou hast returned,"[34] the griffin said.

The boy held up the bowl. "And I learnt."

The griffin examined the roe – alive with its own faint glimmer. "Not taken," it said at last.

"No," the boy answered. "Earned."

The griffin accepted the bowl. Its gold eyes warmed by a

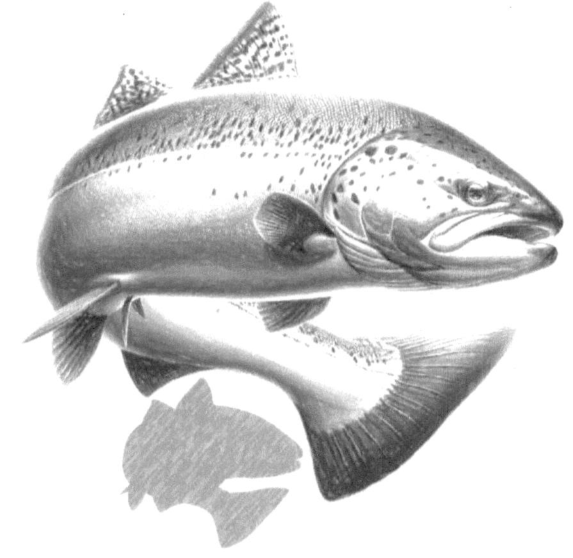

[34] You have returned.

fraction. "And in giving, thou hast received." It bowed its head slightly. "Thou hast passed the first trial, young one. Well done."[35]

Relief flooded through the boy. His knees nearly buckled.

"The second trial awaiteth thee," the griffin continued. "Art thou ready?"[36]

The boy thought about the Blood Tree, alone in the dark. About how much energy the first trial had cost.

"I'm ready."

"Then hear this: Transform the silent white of this kingdom into whispering green."

The boy's mind raced. *Green? In the North?*

"How—"

"That is for thee to discover."[37]

The griffin took the bowl in its claws and opened its wings, already leaning into the air.

"Wait," the boy said. "Do I have time to prepare?"

"Time is thine to use wisely." The griffin paused. "But know this: what thou needest may be closer than thou thinkest."[38]

Then it was gone.

The boy stood alone.

Transform white into green.

He looked at the endless snow. The ice. The frozen wasteland.

How do you grow anything here?

Then his eyes widened.

---

[35] And in giving, you have received. [..] You've passed the first trial, young one. Well done.

[36] The second trial awaits you. [...] Are you ready?

[37] That is for you to discover.

[38] Time is yours to use wisely. [...] But know this: what you need may be closer than you think.

The Blood Tree.

It had grown where nothing should grow, starved of sun and fed by what he'd given, deep underground. Snow did not remain hard around it.

The boy turned back towards the valley. Towards the red leaves in the dark.

"All right," he whispered when he reached the cave. "Show me how."

Chapter XI: The Tides of the Heart

«Beneath the ground and water's spells,
Where fluid silver swims and dwells,
In silent streams that softly flow,
Lie hidden truths the wise shall know.»

The boy returned to the valley.

To the Blood Tree.

It had grown even larger in the time he'd been gone. Its trunk was thick as a barrel now. Its branches spread wide, leaves shimmering like red-crystal in the dim light filtering down.

The boy touched its bark. Warmth pulsed beneath his palm. *We can do this together,* he thought. *You and me.*

He began to expand the cavern even further.

What remained of his wood he fed to the fire. Ice softened and gave way. Water ran in channels he carved, drawn towards the tree's roots.

Then he turned to his magic – not with force, but with stillness.

He stood in deep trance as warmth bled from him into the soil. His breath shortened; the magic pulled, steady and insistent. The tree drank not just magic, but essence – the remembered heat of his mother's hand, his father's steady hold, the summers stored in his bones, the quiet reserves he had never known he carried. He wasn't casting. He was paying. And the price was his own seasons.

The Blood Tree answered. It grew faster.

By nightfall his hands trembled. By morning he could barely stand. Each hour left him lighter, hollowed, as though winter itself had taken up residence inside his bones.

Within a week, the underground chamber had doubled in size. Within two weeks, the tree's canopy brushed the base of the ice pyramid.

The boy lay at its roots afterward, spent – alive, but emptied. When his strength returned, he built supports. He carved vents to draw in air. The cavern changed, slowly, into a greenhouse – warm, humid, alive.

The Blood Tree thrived.

And the boy felt proud.

Beneath the vast canopy, he looked up. *Look at this*, he thought. *We're transforming the North. Making life where there was only ice.*

He imagined the griffin's reaction, him being led onward, towards the North Bear, the trial behind him at last.

In the following weeks, the boy noticed something wrong.

The tree's lower leaves were turning brown.

Not many. Just a few.

He checked the water. The temperature. Everything seemed fine.

Maybe it's just natural. Trees lose leaves.

But more turned brown the next day. And the next.

By the end of the week, whole branches were dying.

The boy panicked.

He used more magic, more warmth. Fed the tree more water.

Nothing helped.

The tree was failing.

The boy sat beneath it, exhausted. Frustrated.

What am I doing wrong?

He'd given everything. Magic. Time. Care. Why wasn't it working? The dying branches creaked above him. And suddenly, the boy understood.

It's alone.

One tree, no matter how he fed it, was still alone. Not a forest. A monument. To *him*.

The realisation hit hard: he was doing it again – forcing life, trying to make will do the work of roots.

The boy looked at the dying Blood Tree.

You need company, he thought. *You need other trees. Other plants. Diversity.*

I can't do this alone. And neither can you.

The boy knew where to go.

East.

To the East Bear.

He climbed out of the valley, his new sleigh in tow. It was rough-made from fallen branches of Blood Tree wood. Beyond the ice pyramid, where dim light funnelled into the cave, he reshaped the sleigh as he walked, wood softening beneath his hands until it fit like a second skin.

By the next day, he reached the ocean.

At the edge of the ice, he changed the wood again. Runners folded inwards. The hull widened. He set out across the restless water.

He crossed the sea, island to island, following the stars. At each stop he gathered wood, adding it to the vessel, refining it: cleaner lines, tighter joints, sails that caught the wind more surely. With every change, it moved faster, as though learning the sea alongside him.

Weeks passed.

Salt cracked his skin. Wind numbed his hands. Each night the vessel demanded more care, more correction, until even small changes left him unsteady. Still, he pressed on.

After more than three weeks on open water, the grey

finally broke.

Green rose on the horizon.

The East.

The bear was waiting at the forest's edge.

As if it had known he was coming.

The boy climbed out of his ship and immediately dropped to his knees.

Not in greeting. In exhaustion. In defeat.

The bear approached slowly.

"Young one," it said gently. "What troubles you?"

The boy's throat was tight.

"I failed. I thought I could... I tried to make a forest from one tree and it's dying and I don't know how to—"

His voice broke.

The bear knelt. Wrapped massive arms around him.

"Breathe," it murmured. "Tell me."

The boy explained. The trial. The Blood Tree. His attempt to transform the North with just one tree.

The bear listened without interrupting. When the boy finished, it was quiet for a long moment.

"I need seeds, please," the boy said.

"Yes... but more than that." The bear rose. "Come."

They walked into the forest, to the river where the Crystal Tree glowed softly. It stood among the strong, green trees, fruit trees and willows, their roots woven together beneath the soil.

"Born of sacrifice. Same as your tree," the bear said, leaning onto the Crystal Tree. The East Bear drove the crystal-tipped staff into the earth. Its light flared softly, not so wild as it used to be, but as if touched by wisdom, steady as a torch. "Fed by love. Yet it does not stand alone."

The bear gestured to the grove around them.

"You are right. Your Blood Tree needs many lives around it. Not to replace it. Only to let it be what it is, without asking it to be everything."

Tears stung the boy's eyes.

"I have seeds," the bear said. "Not mere seeds – offspring of my... of our forest. Hardy, shaped to resist frost and wind. They will stand beside your tree as kin."

The boy stayed three days.

They passed quietly, marked not by hours but by learning. The bear showed him seeds – small, unassuming things, each carrying a different promise. It taught him how to place them in the earth, how depth and spacing mattered, how roots spoke to one another beneath the soil. It told him of balance: of water and shade, of decay and renewal, of how life endured not by force, but by relationship.

When the time came for the boy to leave, the East Bear gathered him into its paws and held him close. The boy felt the great creature's breath against his hair – slow, uneven, almost fragile.

"I wish," the bear murmured, "that the road ahead were gentler for you."

The boy's fingers tightened in its fur.

"And I wish I could stay."

The bear lowered its head until their foreheads touched. For a moment, neither moved.

"You have a world to mend," it whispered. "And wherever your steps may fall, a part of me goes with you."

The boy's breath shivered against its warm chest.

"Come," the bear said softly, pushing itself away from the boy. "There is one more gift."

It lifted its staff, the soft-glowing crystal brushing the boy's brow as lightly as an autumn snowflake. Warmth surged through him, deep and ancient. Images flickered behind his young eyes: old forests rising, falling, returning; roots threading through centuries; the quiet patience of growing things. And the magic in him brightened, answering the staff's call as the crystal dimmed to a final ember.

"This is the legacy of the East," the bear said. "Not strength alone, but memory. With it, you will give more than life to the roots."

The boy knelt and bowed his head, steadying his breath as the power sank deeper into him. The bear laid a gentle paw on his shoulder.

"Rise, young one. The forest walks with you now."

The boy glanced at the dimmed staff. "What will you do without its power?"

The bear shook its head.

"The forest is healed now. It no longer needs my protection. I only need this flicker for one last working."

The boy looked towards the Great Tree, its bark lined with age; still partly grey, still not fully green.

"For the Great Tree? Its roots still hunger."

The bear touched its chest and smiled.

"More than you know. It needs a last spell to drive its roots deeper than any roots have ever gone. To give them more than life." The East Bear leaned on the staff, letting its weight settle. "To give them the memory of you, of me, of all that has been."

"I don't know how to thank you."

"Hug me, young one, and let my heart hold you one more time."

They embraced, warmth held against the cold. Then the bear pressed a letter into his hands. Penned in verdant script, it bore the title "A Short History of the Griffins' Birth".

"Read this when you are ready," it said. "It may help with what comes next."

The boy tucked it into his wood-fibre coat.

The bear's voice caught as it gave its farewell.

"Go," it said. "Transform the North."

The boy turned towards the path ahead, carrying seeds, knowledge, and a promise he did not yet understand. The world widened around him, opening as though the horizon had drawn a deeper breath. Light shimmered with new meaning, alive in every shifting leaf and shadow. And when he moved, a sudden spring rose in his steps, light and startled, alive.

When he neared the edge of sight, the East Bear called softly after him.

"Go forth, young one, bearer of nature's might..."

Its eyes were still wet.

"...my friend. Let it be known that even the humblest heart can bring a season of hope to the coldest winter."

Then the bear turned and walked towards the Great Tree, its steps slow with age.

Before leaving the forest, the boy stopped by the river and embraced the Crystal Tree. His tears slipped into its roots – joy for the mother who had held him close, and sorrow for the one he could no longer reach.

The journey back took three weeks.

The boy arrived at the valley exhausted but determined.

The Blood Tree was still dying. But not dead.

I'm sorry, the boy thought, touching its trunk. *I asked too much of you. But I'm here now. And I brought friends.*

For the next month, he planted the seeds and tended what grew. Seeds from the East Bear, arranged carefully around the Blood Tree. Each placed with intention. Each watered from the luminescent river. The soil darkened and held, ready.

The boy used his magic for them too – not suffering as much as he did for the Blood Tree, but enough. Offering them life was worth the sacrifice.

And slowly, they grew.

Pines. Hardy grasses. Moss. Lichen.

Plants built for cold. For hardship.

They didn't grow as fast as the Blood Tree had. But they grew steadily. Strong.

And as they grew, something changed.

The Blood Tree stopped dying.

Its brown leaves fell. New leaves grew in their place, red-crystalline and bright.

The boy watched in awe as the ecosystem balanced itself.

The smaller plants protected the Blood Tree's roots. The Blood Tree provided shelter, warmth. They fed each other.

Together, the boy thought.

The forest stretched its roots through the thawing earth, reaching towards the returning glow. The entrance to the underground refuge softened in the warmth, and the ice walls that once guarded it began to weep themselves away.

The boy did not falter. He built more.

Expanded the cavern further. Where the old pyramid sagged, he shaped a new shelter of light. Brought sand from distant shores – melted, reformed into glass. Built a dome. Massive. Spanning the cavern. Reinforced it with timber.

From the fallen, melting shards of the pyramid, he carved channels that carried water through the cavern, letting the past feed what was growing now.

He started to speak with the Blood Tree as if to his own child, its branches swaying in quiet answer as his hands moved through the new patterns he had learnt. Later, by the

river, he sat listening to the hum of water over pebbles. A small fear rooted itself in him, sharp and unexpected – the fear that what he loved might one day be undone.

He breathed through it. When he opened his eyes, the river was carving its path with steady certainty. He watched the water find its way around stone and shadow, never stopping, never breaking.

He would be like that, he decided.

Whatever came, he would keep moving forward.

The forest grew.

Not just the Blood Tree. All of it.

Green spreading through the white. Life claiming space in

the ice.

Whispering green, the boy thought, listening to leaves rustle in the warm air.

We did it.

After the third melt-spell, the forest was thriving.

A river ran through it. Trees of a dozen kinds grew strong. The Blood Tree stood at its heart – not dominating, but anchoring. Offering shelter. Offering fruit.

The boy sat beneath it, exhausted but satisfied.

Then remembered: the letter.

He pulled it from his coat. Opened it.

The East Bear's handwriting filled the page.

The first line made his stomach drop.

Chapter XII: Words from the East

«Through winds and storms, 'neath icy charts,
The child bears seeds from distant parts,
To mend the past, his sacred art,
Transforms the world with tides of heart.»

"My Dearest Child,

Your tales of the griffins stirred my curiosity. In the oldest songs of our grove, I found this:

Long ago, gods weakened by curse sought amrita, the seed of light hidden in a primordial sea-dragon's heart. With the asuras' help – shadow-walkers of the border realms – they woke the beast with underwater volcanic fire, tore open its jaws, and retrieved the seed.

But greed turned allies to enemies. The gods prevailed in their strife with the asuras. They drank the amrita's essence and regained their power.

The seed's husk fell to fertile ground, and in time the earth lifted it into a luminous flower of dreams.

From the last two drops of the seed, the gods created a sun-lion, gifted to the asuras in hope of peace, and a flame-bird, kept as their celestial confidant. The Bird of Paradise, they called it; a being of ethereal grace and wisdom, unseen by mortal eyes.

The demons, harbouring old resentment for what they believed was divine treachery, taught the sun-lion to hunt the flame-bird across the heavens. Yet when the great beast rose into the divine spheres, it was undone – not by command, but by love for the Bird of Paradise.

From their union of spirit came seven offspring: griffins, born of wonder, with hearts of stars.

So it is with love, young traveller: a wisp of magic in each chest, and a song the world cannot replace once it is gone.

In the tender dawn of their existence, one offspring wandered from its sanctuary in playful curiosity. A cruel god found it – Nuezuka, whose temper was swift as lightning. In a flash of ire, he transmuted the cub into an astral seed and flung it among the heavens.

From this grew Parijata, a tree of light, its roots and branches spanning all horizons.

Beneath Parijata's distant glow, the sun-lion and flame-bird raised their remaining children in hiding, shielded from the fickle whims of the gods and the lingering malice of the demons.

As I pen these final words, dusk gathers in my chamber, and the stillness keeps me company as the ink dries. Tomorrow you shall be gone, and these feelings shall be all I can give you. Let them light the green cave you seed in the North. The trials are not gates. They are roots you must grow. Remember, my dear child, even in darkness, Parijata's spark binds all that grows.

Until our paths cross once more, I send you all the good fortune you may need in the pursuit of your heart's deepest desires.

With all mine heart,
East Bear."

The boy read it twice before folding the letter. His fingers lingered on the aged parchment, and his throat tightened in a way he didn't have a name for.

The mythology felt distant. Abstract. Beautiful – and, at first, useless. He wanted instructions. A lever. A shortcut.

Why had the bear sent this?

He tucked the letter away, and looked at his forest. At his Blood Tree glowing under the distant light.

Like Parijata.

And then it struck him.

The letter wasn't about the past at all. It was about the griffins – about *this.*

They weren't merely guardians, he realised.

Each trial was more than a test: patience, kinship, the slow work of becoming, and the courage to stand together against whatever sought to break them.

That's what they're teaching me. Not to prove I'm worthy. To become worthy. My hands keep curling into fists before I remember what I'm trying to build.

Footsteps crunched in snow above. The boy stood, dusted off his clothes, and climbed out of the cavern.

Outside, a griffin was waiting. The third. Its feathers had green tints at the edges, like spring pressing through winter. Snow-plume still clung to it, thrown up by its landing, or by the gale that broke around it in a white roar.

The boy tilted his head back and shaded his eyes, searching up and up for the creature's crown. His shadow, a small blot beneath the griffin's, seemed to shrink.

The griffin shook the snow from its wings, looked at him, then past him towards the dome that covered the forest.

The boy gathered his breath. "Great Griffin—"

The griffin lowered its head, bringing its gaze level with his. Its breath struck the boy full in the chest. He trembled, wordless.

"Tell me, little leaf," the griffin huffed. "Thou hast brought green to white," it said. "We all felt it. How came this to be?"[39]

"Not alone," the boy answered, steadying himself. "With help."

The griffin's eyes gleamed. "Show me."

He led the creature closer and revealed the forest beneath ice and glass.

The griffin's breath misted the dome for a long while before it finally turned to him.

"Thou hast not wrought this with one tree."[40]

"No. I tried. It failed."

The griffin regarded him for a long moment, gaze sharp as ice.

"And what did thy failure teach thee?"[41]

"That I kept trying to force the world," the boy said, the words scraping out of him. "Breaking almost everything I touched."

He swallowed.

"That one tree was not enough. Even a special one needs others to become a forest."

The griffin's feathers rippled once, like a thought passing through a body.

"Good," it said.

Then the third griffin raised its head towards the clouds. "Very well. Green without voice is half-born. Wake it."

The boy blinked. "Wake it..."

"Make thy green realm whisper. Give it breath: wind that moveth by its own will, and voices that live here without

---

[39] Tell me, little leaf. You have brought green to white. We all felt it. How did you do it?

[40] You haven't done this with one tree.

[41] And what did your failure teach you?

thee."[42] The griffin's gaze burned bright.

"How—"

"That is thy trial to bear." It spread its wings. "Return when thy forest speaketh – before the next aurora tide leaveth the sky."[43] Then it was gone in a rush of white wind.

Riddles again, the boy thought, brushing snow from his shoulders. *And always the clock.*

Then he went back below to his forest, looking at the Blood

---

[42] Make your green realm whisper. Give it breath: wind that moves by its own will, and voices that live here without you.

[43] That is your trial to bear. [...] Return when your forest speaks, before the next aurora season leaves the sky.

Tree and the companions growing around it. He lifted a hand towards the canopy.

For a breath, the leaves trembled.

Then the air fell dead again.

Two trials down, he thought. *Two to go.*

He was tired; the wand-magic in him lay like an ember under ash, and his bones remembered every mile of ice.

But he was learning.

And that was worth everything.

Tomorrow, he would go down to the river and listen until the water taught him a language the leaves could speak.

The realm's pale light shimmered over his skin, and his new forest answered only with listening shadows.

Only the unabated river kept speaking, running its old language under the ice.

Chapter XIII: The Third Stood Still

«Guided by words from eastern realm,
The child finds stories at the helm.
Through ancient echoes, paths embark,
He moulds his future with tales stark.»

Make the forest sing.

The boy looked up at the dome. Far off, the sky began to colour, faint and hesitant. The third griffin's words ticked in his ribs.

The Blood Tree's red-crystal leaves. The companions from the eastern forest growing strong.

But silent. No *living* sound. Only the wind sliding through leaves.

He sat down in the centre of the forest and listened.

Just wind. And his breathing.

I can make them speak to me. Make them like me.

The thought tasted familiar: *control first, understand later.* Yet he spent two days trying. He pushed magic into their trunks, willing them towards sound. Nothing. Or worse – a creaking like wood splitting. Wrong.

Maybe they need to learn how to speak. I can use wind to teach them. I can learn their leaves' language, their feelings.

He shaped the air into currents, guiding it through branches and crystal leaves until a clean note rose – leaf against leaf, wind made audible for a heartbeat.

It worked – briefly. The moment his focus slipped, the sound died. It felt like his doing, not the trees'.

He tried again, harder this time, forcing the idea of a voice into the trees.

This was the worst attempt of all.

When he pushed magic into the Blood Tree, it screamed – a high, tearing sound that rang in his skull. Like a terrified child discovering its voice could bleed into the wind before it even knew what words were.

He cut the magic at once, stumbling back.

The leaves shivered, agitated.

I'm sorry, he thought, pressing his hand to the trunk. *I'm so sorry.*

He pressed his fists against his head, exhausted and frustrated. His head ached. He was forcing the trees to be something that they weren't ready to be. *Wrong again*, he realised. But what were the choices?

Where does sound come from in a forest?

Not from magic forcing it. From... life itself. From trees and creatures. From community.

The South Bear.

The thought arrived with certainty.

The South Bear created life from cocoa. Breathed it into being. Its kingdom was full of sound – creatures singing, moving, living.

That's where I need to go.

The boy climbed out of the forest.

Once again, he reshaped the sleigh-sphere, sealing it close about his body.

A day later, when the ice gave way to sea, he unfolded the wooden shell into a mechanised watercraft and turned the prow south.

As he rowed away from the North, shame burned in his chest. *When will I ever get it right?*

Then, beneath the sting, a quieter truth surfaced: the trials weren't about perfection at all, but about learning what "right" even meant. He needed that.

He rowed faster.

Towards the South Bear – towards help.

The journey southward took six weeks – long enough to replay his failure, long enough to feel the weight of needing help again. But when the chocolate island finally rose through the fog, relief washed over him. He was tired of being alone with his inadequacy.

The clean sting of mint on the air, the springs running clear where he'd once spilled them – all of it waiting for him. At the shore stood the South Bear, as if it had been part of everything. And when it saw him approaching, the bear bounded into the water, laughing.

"Hark! My runaway north-wanderer returns. Welcome back, my friend... I almost feared the frost had claimed you."

The boy climbed out of his watercraft, exhausted.

The bear swept him into a hug that lifted him off his feet.

"I've missed you," the boy murmured, his voice muffled against fur, a faint chocolate warmth rising in his throat.

The bear held him tighter. *Me too*, its thought echoed inside the boy's mind – a familiar brush behind the ear, warm as cocoa breath.

"My liege," the boy said, finding his feet. "I need your help."

"Of course you do!" The bear turned swiftly, hiding the spark of tears before adding, "That's what friends are for. Come! Food first, crisis second. That's the rule."

On the way to the palace, the boy nibbled mint-chocolate twigs and gingerbread stones, then scooped warm milk-chocolate into his cupped hands and drank, taking care not to harm a single thing.

The whimsical bear chattered on about how he had made

everything stronger, drifting into another absurd story – the time it tried to teach the muffin-dragons to juggle. The boy laughed until his sides ached, until tears blurred his vision, until he forgot where he was and why he'd come...

Then he stopped. All at once – like a string snapped inside his ribs, the body left out of tune.

The South Bear paused mid-gesture. *What's wrong?*

"I..." The boy's face crumpled. "I can't. I can't do this."

"Do what?"

"Be happy. Laugh. Feel..." He gestured helplessly at the sweet forest, at the joy surrounding them. "Feel good. Everyone I loved is gone. And I'm... here eating chocolate rivers and laughing at jokes and it's... it's wrong. It's disrespectful. It's..."

"It's being alive," the South Bear said gently. *Grief doesn't mean you surrender all joy because the one who passed away can't feel it anymore. That's not love. That's... that's revenge. Revenge on yourself. Grief always finds a place to fall.*

The bear's thoughts were kind; yet they left a restless tremor in him.

"It hurts," the boy whispered. "It hurts to feel good."

"I know," the bear said softly. "There is an ache that follows some who live on, like a wound that flares whenever joy dares to return." *It's real. It's hard. But it's also a bit selfish... a way of punishing yourself, as if pain could prove your love*. The bear winced apologetically.

The boy jerked back.

"What are you afraid of?" The bear turned to him.

"I'm afraid..." His voice was small. "I'm afraid that if I'm happy, it means it didn't matter. That losing love didn't matter."

"Ah." The South Bear nodded. "But the opposite is true. If

you refuse joy forever, if you make yourself miserable to prove a point... then you carry death inside." *Is that what you want?* The thought cut sharp.

"No."

"Then give yourself permission, my friend. Permission to heal. Permission to laugh. Permission to eat ridiculous amounts of chocolate and tell bad jokes and... feel good sometimes." The bear tapped the boy's chest. "Everyone who is gone lives in here. And they want you to be happy. Trust me."

Then the bear turned and walked away, as softly as a creature its size could manage, giving the boy space to breathe.

The boy stood there, staring at the space where the South Bear had been.

For a long moment, he didn't move.

"Come on," the bear's voice nudged him. "You're not planning on becoming a statue, are you?"

The breath he'd been holding shuddered out of him. His knees bent, not collapsing, just... softening. He pressed a hand to his chest, feeling the ache and the warmth tangled together there.

"Coming," he finally said.

The South Bear's ears twitched as the boy ran to catch up, but it didn't turn. It simply slowed its great stride by a fraction. When the boy fell into step beside it, the bear let out a soft hum, low and warm, a small smile tugging at the corner of its muzzle.

"Better," it murmured. "Statues are dreadful company. They never laugh at my jokes. Not even at the good ones."

The boy huffed a breath that might have been a laugh. The bear pretended not to notice, padding forward through the warm, cocoa-toned trees. But the boy felt it: the tiniest shift inside him, like a door cracked open to let in air. Somewhere far off, a sweet bird chirped, its voice quick and alive.

And when they reached the throne room, they found a feast laid out in their honour, steaming, piled high, and prepared with far too much enthusiasm. The boy ate: caramel, pudding, hot chocolate, meringue, pies, things he couldn't even name. His body needed it. He'd been burning magic and eating little for weeks.

The South Bear watched him with knowing eyes. At last, when the fire settled in the famished boy, the bear's thought found his mind. *Tell me.*

So the boy told him. The trial. The forest. His attempts to force sound into being with magic alone.

"Nothing worked," he finished, voice small. "I tried everything. But it all felt... forced. Artificial. Wrong."

The bear nodded slowly. *And? What did you learn?*

"That I can't do it with magic."

"Mm. Close. But not quite." The bear rose and padded to its work table. *Come here.* The boy joined it.

The bear scooped a handful of cocoa powder and breathed on it. A chocolate bird gathered itself from the dust. It fluttered into shape, wings beating softly, then chirped – a crisp, living sound – before darting through the ceiling tunnels and out of sight.

"Did you hear that?" the bear asked.

"The chirp?"

"Yes. That sound didn't come from me. It came from the bird. From its life."

The boy frowned. "But you created it."

"I gave it form. But its voice? That's its own." *Living things make sound the way they breathe. You can't force it.* The bear's eyes settled on him. "Your forest needs that. Things that sing because they're alive, because they *want to*, not because you force them to exist."

The boy stared at the table, at the cocoa powder waiting to become something.

"I don't know how to do that."

"I know." The bear reached into its cloak and drew out a small golden cup, carved with intricate patterns. "That's why you should use this."

The cup was beautiful. Delicate, but solid in his hands.

"What does it do?"

"It measures," the bear said, smiling. "Not power – *permission*. Used with magic, it helps you offer life a doorway without deciding what must walk through."

The boy held it carefully. "Why now?"

Before you weren't ready. You hadn't learnt the difference between shaping a world... and owning it. The thought struck deep as it settled in the boy's mind.

"You needed to try alone first," the bear continued. "To understand that creation isn't about power. It's about invitation. Joy. Making space for something new to exist."

The boy looked down at the cup, at his reflection wavering in its golden surface.

"There's more," the bear said quietly. It placed a paw on the boy's chest, directly over his heart. Warmth surged through him. Not magic. Something older. Deeper.

The boy gasped. "What—"

"A gift," the bear said. *My heart's rhythm, woven into yours. So you'll remember: joy creates. Fear destroys. And true sound can only come from true life.*

But the boy almost didn't hear the bear's thoughts. The warmth settled inside him, pulsing gently – a second heartbeat beneath his own.

His eyes stung. “Thank you,” he managed.

“Don’t thank me yet.” The bear’s expression shifted, the lightness falling away. “There’s something you must understand. About the griffins. And about why sound matters to them more than anything.”

They sat together.

“After the griffins were born,” the bear began, “the demons shaped monsters of their own – cyclopes, born from vengeful darkness. War came soon after.” Its paws were restless as it spoke. “The cyclopes were defeated, yes... but defeat didn’t tame them. In retreat they fled like fire, leaving charred hollows behind.

“The flame-bird never returned to its nest. Slaughtered while foraging for the young.

“The sun-lion avenged it, slew many cyclopes, and came back bleeding light. Mortally wounded.”

The bear’s voice softened.

“With its last strength, the sun-lion guided its young northward, to those frozen lands – though they were green then. Warm. Alive. And on its deathbed, it gave its children a final gift: the last drop of amrita, the seed of light that had kept its heart alive.”

The boy leaned in.

“The griffins planted that seed, and from it grew the White Tree.”

His breath caught. “The White Tree?”

“Their father’s legacy,” the bear said. “The heart of the northern realm. It held magic – healing, truth, life itself.”

A quiet settled between them before the bear went on.

“But humans came, driven mad by a curse from dying cyclopes. Greed infected them. They attacked the griffins for the tree's power. War flared again... and when it ended, the White Tree was gone. And the North went quiet, as if the world had lost its heart."

The boy was trembling. "The Blood Tree..."

"Yes." The bear's eyes darkened with sorrow. "Your Blood Tree echoes the White Tree. Born from your blood. From your sacrifice. It holds memory – yours, and the land's." *That is why the griffins care so deeply for your forest. It is not merely green in white. It is their father's memory, alive again.*

The thought landed clean in the boy's mind. He couldn't speak.

"Sound matters," the bear continued, "because the White Tree sang. Gave life. Its leaves made music. When it died, the North fell silent. The griffins have been waiting centuries for someone to bring that song back."

The boy understood now. This wasn't just a trial.

It was healing.

He stayed two more days.

In that time, the bear taught him to use the cup – not to command life, but to welcome it. To shape possibility, not outcome.

It was far more difficult than he expected. Each attempt tightened his jaw, his instinct always to control, to force the creature into the exact form he imagined.

No, the bear would chide gently. *Offer it shape. Then let it choose.*

At last, the boy managed one: a small chocolate bird. It rose from the cocoa, shook itself free, blinked at him with bright curiosity – and chirped.

Real. Clear. Alive.

The boy laughed, startled by the sound.

"There," the bear said, grinning. "That's the sound."

When the morning of his departure came, the bear walked him to the shore. Together they loaded the watercraft with cocoa, tools, and things he'd need for the journey ahead.

Then the bear embraced him. Long. Tight.

"You'll do well," it murmured. "You have my heart now. Let it guide you."

The boy buried his face in the bear's fur. "I don't want to leave."

"I know. But the North needs you. The griffins need you." The bear drew back, its expression turning solemn. "And you need to finish this. You've learnt to surrender, to face darkness, to die and be reborn. Those were hard lessons."

The bear smiled gently. "But joy, lightness, the permission to heal... that may be the hardest of all. Because it means being someone who lost his mother and his father – yet is defined by that loss no longer."

"I'm scared I don't know how to be that person."

"You don't," the bear agreed. "Not yet. But you're learning."

It leaned down and kissed his forehead. "Go north, child. But remember: wisdom without joy is a road that never warms your feet. Real wisdom knows when to be solemn... and when to eat cake."

The boy laughed bitterly. Couldn't speak past the lump in his throat.

"Go," the bear said gently. "Make the forest sing. Then come back and tell me about it."

The boy climbed into his watercraft. Looked back once.

The bear was watching. Paw raised.

The boy waved. Then rowed north. Carrying the cup. The South Bear's heartbeat inside. And understanding.

"Off you go, brave little traveller," it called. "My den stays open – no matter how far you..." Its voice drifted into the forest's shadow as tears gathered in its eyes, this time not born of joy. It dabbed its whiskers dry, drew a steadying breath.

The child was already fading into the distance.

The bear lifted its paw one last time, and let its thought drift over the ocean. *Farewell, my child. Go make the North sing.*

It stood still for a few moments. Then it turned away, leaving only the memory of its warmth behind.

Chapter XIV: The Long Way Back

«Amid legends deep where griffins dwell,
The third stood still, under their spell.
With courage sown in each brave start,
He weaves the fabric of his art.»

The journey back took longer than before.

The boy used the time to practise.

Each night, he'd stop at one of the black-rock stepping-islands that freckled this sea like spilled ink, pull out the cup, and try to coax small creatures from wood, stone, sand. Offer shape – never a command – so whatever came could choose to stay. Most attempts failed. The magic bucked, slipped, scattered. He tried harder, jaw clenched.

And that was when the old memory rose – not summoned, but triggered.

He was five again – rain on wood. A narrow bridge behind his parents' house. Slick boards flexing over a ditch that felt like a river when you were small enough to believe shallow water could take you.

His small hands gripping the rope too tightly. His mother lifting a dough-fish with currant eyes, turning fear into play with a gesture so simple it felt like magic. His father's voice drifting through the bridge's wobbles: "Feel it. Lean into it. Let the bridge move and you move with it. Find your balance."

And he did. He felt his shaking, the bridge's sway, the rain. He saw a droplet sliding from his sleeve and vanishing into the restless water. Yet he loosened his grip – not letting go, just not clinging. The bridge steadied. So did he.

He crossed. His mother pressed the warm bowl into his

hands like a crown. His father ruffled his hair and said "Brave," as if bravery were something you learnt by doing.

Even then he knew: you don't cross and remain the same. Something soft is left behind. Something steadier walks off.

The memory thinned, leaving him with its lesson. He focused – unclenched his jaw, and let the cup rest in his palm instead of gripping it like a tool.

The South Bear's heartbeat pulsed beneath his own, steady as his father's voice had been.

It didn't come all at once. One night a beetle clicked on the rim of the cup – *not because he asked it to, but because it had decided the world was worth answering.*

After that, the first birds followed. By the time he reached the North, he could create small lives that chose their own sounds. Almost perfect. Real enough.

He descended into the cave's forest. He stood in its centre and looked up at the Blood Tree.

I came back different, he thought. *So I'll ask differently.*

He pulled out the cup.

Filled it with cocoa from the South Bear. With wood shavings, petals and leaves from the trees around him. Mixed them. Then he used magic to invite.

Come, he thought. *There's room here – no hooks, no chains. Only shelter, if you choose it.*

The cocoa stirred. Rose from the cup. Took shape.

A bird. Small. Wooden body. Chocolate and petals for feathers. Bright eyes.

It perched on the cup's rim and looked at him.

Chirped. The note struck the leaves and the dome's glass and returned changed – warmer, multiplied, as the trees answered with their first, faint shiver.

The boy's eyes burned.

"Welcome," he whispered.

The bird flew to a branch. Nested there. Kept singing.

He created more.

Not quickly. Each one took time. Energy. Care.

Birds came first: small, bright arguments against the silence. Then the undergrowth began to move: beetles that clicked like pebbles, bees that stitched the air, a pine-cone turtle that dragged its slow patience through moss.

Not an army. A neighbourhood.

Root-spined and bark-scaled, leaf-crested little lives came to be: amber eyes glinting, bark-sliver tongues tasting the air, moving over knotted roots and fallen branches with willow-flexed bodies and leaf-padded toes, as though they had always belonged.

Each chose its own sound.

Wings fluttering. Feet scurrying. Voices calling. The forest filled. Not with forced magic. With life.

By the end of the week, the boy was exhausted. His magic almost completely depleted. The South Bear's heartbeat in his chest thinned, not vanishing – just quieter, as if the bear's laugh was drifting farther away now, trusting him to finish the last step alone.

But the forest was singing.

He lay beneath the Blood Tree, listening.

Birdsong from above. Insects humming. Small creatures rustling through undergrowth.

A symphony.

He watched wooden squirrels flit through the branches and wondered whether this realm would remember him when he'd be gone, whether his joy would live on in others. Amid the living chorus, he stood there with sap on his fingers and tears he didn't bother wiping – too full to speak, too tired to pretend he wasn't. Drained and full at once, as only those who make something true ever are.

The boy closed his eyes.

Thank you, he thought – to the South Bear, to the creatures, to the forest itself.

We did it together.

He climbed out of the cavern.

Made his way back to the palace. A smile crossed his blue-tinged lips, mingling with the sting of warm tears, as he approached the gate.

The fourth griffin waited where the wind died. White, vast, edged in a faint gold that didn't gleam so much as remember gleaming.

It descended when it saw him.

"The third trial," the boy said. "It's complete. The forest sings."

The griffin's eyes glowed. "Show me."

They walked to the valley together. The griffin was massive. Its footsteps shook the ground. But it moved with surprising grace.

When they reached the dome, the griffin stopped.

Listened.

Even from outside, the sounds were audible. Muffled by glass but unmistakable.

Birdsong. Insect hum. Life.

The boy stopped before the wooden entry to the dome. At his touch, the roots loosened and drew back, thick cords of wood uncoiling with low creaks. Branches folded inwards and upwards, leaves whispering as they parted, until the great opening widened, yielding as though the forest itself were making room. The boy expanded it as large as he could, without damaging the structure. Then he stepped in. The griffin lowered its head through it with a care so precise it felt like reverence.

The forest greeted them with sound. Birds called from branches. Insects darted through shafts of light. Small creatures froze, watching the enormous griffin, then scattered.

The ancient creature did not move, as if motion itself might have disturbed what it was seeing. It listened not just to the sounds, but to the silences between them. The boy had seen wind shift under magic. But this was different: stillness chosen, as if the world were being asked to listen properly.

The griffin's eyes moved slowly, taking in the Blood Tree at the centre, the forest growing around it, the creatures filling every space. Its shadow stretched across the entry and most of the dome, vast and sheltering. Its talons brushed the dome, careful not to mar what lived there.

The shadow of its large claws passed over the boy's face. He traced the faint claw scar along his cheek. Part of him ached – the part that had gone into the making and would not return. The forest was fuller for it. He was quieter.

And in that imbalance, he felt how closely ambition and tenderness were bound, how both asked you to give before they gave back.

Only then did he understand: the ache in his cheek, the sap on his hands, the quiet inside him – this was the cost of choosing well. Not once. Again and again. Even when no one was watching.

"Tell me, spirit of the green," the old griffin said, its voice low, as though speaking to something long-forgotten within the Blood Tree, "what magic kindleth this place?"[44]

---

[44] Tell me, forest, what magic gives this place life?

It fell silent. The boy looked at the griffin, thinking the words were meant for him. Then he understood, and said nothing.

"I am humbled by thee," the griffin whispered at last, like waking up from a dream. "By all thy harmonies."[45]

Its wings stirred, slow and heavy.

"May thy voice endure in our hearts."[46]

It opened its eyes, and turned its beak to the boy.

"How?"

"I created them," the boy said. "With help. And with permission: mine, and theirs."

He hesitated.

"They chose to sing. To be here."

A breath.

"My magic only opened the door."

"And so it is." The griffin closed its eyes. Listened.

When it opened them again, they were wet.

"This sound," it said, its voice worn, "is the last memory we have of the White Tree. Before it fell. Before silence took the North."

The boy's throat tightened.

"I never thought I should hear it again," said the old griffin.

It bowed its head.

"Thou hast passed the third trial. More than passed. Thou hast healed that which we long believed lost."[47]

The boy couldn't speak.

They stood there, lost in the forest's sounds, for a long time.

---

[45] I'm humbled by you, [...] by all your harmonies.
[46] May your voice endure in our hearts.
[47] You have passed the third trial. More than passed. You have healed what we long believed [was] lost.

Finally, the griffin straightened.

"One trial yet remaineth,"[48] it said. "The final test, set by Its Majesty itself."

The boy nodded. "I'm ready."

"Art thou?" Its gaze was steady, unblinking. "This trial shall not weigh thy skill, nor thy wisdom. It shall weigh thy heart."[49]

The boy's chest tightened. "What does that mean?"

"Thou wilt know when the hour cometh. Follow me. The

---

48 One trial remains.

49 Are you [ready]? [...] This trial will not measure your skill or your wisdom. It will measure your heart.

King awaiteth."[50]

They walked back to the palace. And when they reached it, the doors opened with a sound like a glacier admitting it had been moving all along.

The griffin gestured with one wing. "The waves have shaped the cliff. Step forth, child of the frost, and let thy heart lead thee farther. The throne room lieth at the passage's end."[51]

The boy looked up at the doors. At his reflection in their icy surface.

One more trial.

He'd failed and learnt. Failed and grown.

Whatever it is, I can face it.

He took a breath.

Stepped through the doors.

Into the palace.

Towards whatever waited.

---

[50] You will know when the hour comes. Follow me. The King awaits.

[51] The waves have shaped the cliff. Step forth, child of the frost, and let your heart lead you farther. The throne room lies at the passage's end.

Chapter XV: Within

«Guided by stars and moon's soft light,
In realms of frost, his spirit bright.
With griffins' wings and the bears' lore
A journey turns through palace doors.»

Inside the palace was cold. Not uncomfortable. Just... aware. Like the ice itself was watching.

The boy walked slowly. His footsteps echoed.

The walls were carved with images: cyclopes, griffins, trees from warmer seasons he didn't recognise. Scenes of battles. Of peace. Of something being built and destroyed and built again.

He passed through corridor after corridor, and each one drew him deeper – not only into the palace, but into something else. Into the part of him that kept walking, he realised.

Memories rose as he walked.

His mother's funeral. The smell of lilies. Rain on stone. The air of that day had been heavy with stillness, the sky washed in muted greys.

His father's face, blurred now, as if grief had rubbed it with its thumb. Somewhere, a bell tolled, distant as a different life.

The golden beach. Snowy. The door that had brought him here.

The leviathan's teeth. Drowning. Surrender.

Being stone. Being wood. Being reborn.

The East Bear's tears. The South Bear's laughter.

He had been someone's son. Then alone. Then a seeker, a student, a creator.

He stopped. Cold crept through the soles of his shoes.

Before him stood the doors. Massive. Crystal. Holding his reflection.

The boy stared.

Thin. Scarred. Eyes older than they should have been.

The image wavered.

For a moment, he did not know whether what he saw was what remained, or what had replaced him.

The thought passed.

He breathed and pressed his half-open hand to the crystal. His reflection pushed back.

The doors did not ask his name. They opened to a vast throne room.

The ceiling disappeared into darkness. Thousands of lights glowed above – stars, trapped in ice, casting everything in soft white-blue.

The air was different here. Warmer than it should be, thick with frost and fur, salt and feather: land, sea, and sky held in a single breath.

Animals filled the room.

Hundreds of them. Thousands.

Wolves. Foxes. Bears. Seals. Caribou. Birds perched on ice formations. Fish visible through transparent floor sections. Predator and prey passing one another without instinct or fear, as if the room had borrowed them, and meant to return them later.

All watching him.

They parted as he walked, creating a path, heads dipping, throats going still, as if the air itself had asked for silence.

At the far end: a throne.

And on the throne: the North Bear.

It looked like *Snowy*. For one heartbeat, something in him

surged forward, so fast it hurt. Then he saw the differences. Larger. Older. Eyes deeper. Scars hidden beneath white fur.

Not Snowy. But similar enough to hurt.

The boy walked forward slowly.

The bear watched him approach. Its eyes were impossibly old, as though they had watched many shapes pass and never needed to remember them.

When the boy stopped before the throne, the bear spoke.

Not aloud. The words appeared in the boy's mind with the sound of snowflakes falling.

Welcome, child of wandering stars.

Yet as the North Bear's thoughts found him, everything shifted. It was as if he had stepped through a cloud. Suddenly, there was no ice now, no cold. The animals' thoughts unfolded around him – *not as words*, but as meaning, immediate and complete. The space had softened, filled with warm currents and unfamiliar light, everything distant and near at the same time.

Forms shifted.

Creatures stretched and thinned, collapsed and widened, dwindled to nothing and swelled beyond measure. Shapes flowed into one another, fitting or clashing, while distance itself bent and unravelled, shrinking to absence, then opening into vastness.

There was no colour – no shadow either, not in any way eyes could name. And yet colour was everywhere, felt rather than seen, as though it had slipped free of shape.

The space folded and turned, twisting like a ball of yarn. A dance he somehow knew.

It was strange.

It was familiar.

And the North Bear's thoughts stretched through all,

formed and unformed, as if time were a mere concept revealed by the pull of the threads.

Welcome to the space where wanting is louder than having, the bear's thought unfurled. *Here, every desire takes shape, close enough to taste, then slips away before it can satisfy. Keep breathing it in and you will forget where you end.*

We have built empires of longing here. They all collapse inwards, into the same hunger. Always.

We do not need another noun, child. We need a verb.

The thoughts crashed and rolled like waves against any beginning or end. Yet the bear's eyes were warm, almost tender.

Can you give us that verb? asked the bear inside the boy's fluid mind. *For we are starving, dear boy.*

"Your Majesty." The boy's voice was small when he finally found it. The air thickened. Colours bled into unfamiliar rules. The bear's form blurred at the edges. The boy's vision swam. *What's happening?*

This is the space between, the bear's thoughts echoed. *Between what you are and what you might become. Between form and formlessness.*

"I passed three trials, learnt patience, collaboration, creation. Isn't that... *enough*?"

His words rolled through the air and broke into a low, swelling roar. They scattered as silver fish, turning as one, drawn back towards the sea that had cast them onto the shore.

The bear regarded the child's words with patience. With its reply, the silver fish lifted, reshaping into birds – broad-winged, leaf-veined, their bodies scaled with living green. They rose and vanished into the light.

"Oh," the bear intoned, its voice a low rumble, words catching the air like claws, "that was only a drop of salt in the

brine."

It paused.

"We hunger for more," the bear said. "So give us what we need – whole, or not at all."

"What shall I give?"

The bear's gaze fixed on him. Its eyes, dark with something older than thought, narrowed to a single point. "Your heart."

The boy's breath stopped. All the creatures' eyes turned to him.

"My... what?" He tried to focus. Failed. Everything was fluid. Unstable.

We ask for your heart, the bear's thoughts settled clear in the boy's chest. *What will you give?*

The boy's mind raced.

His heart? His memories? His feelings? His life?

"If you don't know, let your desire choose," the bear said, and the boy felt the room tighten, as if every creature had taken the same breath and refused to spend it. Two objects formed in the air before him: a golden chalice and a small diamond dish.

"Two offerings," the bear said, observing the objects as if tasting their meaning. "The chalice takes one memory, core and load-bearing, and leaves you with clarity where your mind has only fog. Or the dish takes feeling itself: joy, grief, love, fear, drained until you can name every syllable, and none of it moves you. What shall it be?"

The boy stared.

Neither choice felt right. To lose a memory was to erase himself. To lose all feeling was to vanish. There had to be another way.

"I..." His voice cracked. "I don't want to give up pieces of myself."

Then what will you give?

His hands clenched.

What was truly his to give?

Not his memories. They had been shaped by others. Not his feelings. They rose and fell on their own.

His heart was... the verb. Not the thing itself. The sharing of it.

To tell.

The thought arrived whole.

He looked up at the bear.

"I'll give you my whole heart," he said. "Not by cutting it out. By sharing it. Completely."

The bear's eyes widened slightly as the world settled back into shape, the infinite pouring into now.

"Let me tell you everything," the boy said. "Every memory, feeling. Every moment that made me who I am."

And then?

"Then you'll have my heart," he said. "Because you'll know me."

The bear was silent a long moment.

Then: *Yes.*

But do you know the cost?

"To be fully known," the bear continued, "is to risk everything. To stand without defence. To die, in a way."

The boy's hands trembled.

He had died before. And returned.

"I understand," he whispered. "I'm ready."

The bear nodded.

Then speak, child. And let us see if you survive the story.

And if you lie – if you flinch from your own truth – this space will keep you unfinished. You shall leave with your shape, but not your centre.

The boy took a breath.

And began.

Chapter XVI: The Last Song

«A dance of light, of shadows intertwined,
A boy steps forth, his destiny defined.
With heart in hand, into the vast unknown,
Where stars guide him to where his light is shown.»

The boy spoke.

Not in sentences. In images. In feelings.

Each memory left his mouth the way breath leaves glass – fogging the air, then clearing, as if the room itself had to make space for what he carried.

He began with his first memory: his mother's voice. Warm. Safe. The last time he had felt whole.

Then his father. Faded. Gone too soon. A hole that never filled.

His mother's illness. Watching her fade. Not understanding why. Her death. The funeral. Adults who could not look at him.

Being alone.

The door. The choice to leave.

The golden beach and Snowy, playing in the sun.

As he spoke, the boy moved. Not dancing. Not quite. His body swayed. His hands gestured. His face contorted with remembered pain, remembered joy.

He told of the pirates. The ocean. The old man.

The Fairy Queen and her gift, the wand. The confrontation with his shadow.

The leviathan's teeth. The drowning. The surrender. His voice broke. But he kept going.

The East Bear. The petrification. The terror of darkness.

The Crystal Tree. Twelve years of singing. Rebirth. The cost. The innocence lost.

"I forgot everything. Became nothing. Then came back changed. The world aged twelve years without me. Will anyone remember her at all?"

The South Bear. The chocolate island. Destruction. Shame.

"I broke it. Then I stayed. I cleaned up what I'd done. That, more than magic, was growing."

The salmon. The Blood Tree. Patience. The forest growing. Life from sacrifice.

"The tree gave me purpose. We are bound now."

The griffins and the trials. Failure after failure. Learning.

Slowly. Painfully.

Hours passed – measured only by the roughening of his throat and the way his legs stopped feeling like his own. His body shook with exhaustion, each step a refusal. But he did not stop.

Every memory. Every feeling. Every shame and pride and fear.

The animals watched. Silent. The bear's eyes never left him.

As the boy neared the end, his movements became frantic. Desperate. Tired. Like a dance. He was giving everything. Holding nothing back.

"This is me," he said. "All of it." *The scared and the brave. The broken and the healing.* His thought reached for the North Bear's heart. Found only its eyes.

"That's how I came here. Now. Giving you everything." His voice fell to a whisper. His legs gave out. He hit the ice hard. Tried to breathe – and found nothing to pull. Like his lungs had forgotten the shape of air.

He had given all.

I'm dying. The thought floated a step behind him, as if it belonged to someone else. The room thinned. Sound became snow. Even fear grew quiet. The last thing he saw was the North Bear rising from its throne. His vision darkened.

And he was alone again – *not in the room, but somewhere behind it.*

The ice castle stood before him, its doors thrown wide. No griffin.

Only Snowy, walking beside him.

"Wait." Snowy grabbed his arm as they reached the crystal gates.

"What?" the boy asked.

The bear's eyes were wide. Afraid. Truly afraid. "We can't go in there."

"What do you mean, Snowy?"

"The North Bear's magic... it's too strong. It would—"

Snowy's paws trembled. "I can't go."

"No." The boy shook his head. "We do this together."

"But—"

"What if I need you?" His voice rose. "What if something goes wrong and you're not there? What if I can't find my way back?"

"You will." Snowy's voice was gentle. Certain. "You're strong enough now."

"I don't feel strong."

"I know." Snowy pressed a paw to the boy's chest. "The strong ones never do. But I'm here. I've been here since your mother gave me to you. I'm not just outside anymore, cub. I'm inside too."

Tears filled the boy's eyes. "That's not enough. I need you real. I need—"

"I know." Snowy pulled him close. "But sometimes we have to do hard things alone. That's part of growing. That's part of surviving."

"I don't want to survive without you."

"You won't."

Snowy pulled back, met his eyes.

"Trust that I'll be here when you come out."

The boy wiped his face.

"Okay."

"And when it gets hard – and it will – remember this: you've never been alone. Your mother's in you. The bears are in you. And I..."

Snowy's voice faltered.

The boy hugged it. Tight.

Then let it go slowly. Turned towards the gates.

He didn't look back.

Snowy watched until the boy disappeared. Then it sat in the snow and waited, as toys do, with infinite patience and infinite love.

Warmth touched the boy's face.

His eyes fluttered.

Am I—

Breath filled his lungs. Not his own.

He gasped. Choked. His chest convulsed.

Life surged back. He opened his eyes.

The North Bear knelt beside him. Its massive paw pressed against the boy's chest. *Breathe.*

He did. Ragged. Painful. Each breath scraped its way back.

"What... happened?"

"You died," the bear said simply. "Gave your heart so completely you forgot to keep breathing."

The boy stared up at it.

"I brought you back."

The bear's eyes were deep. Unfathomable.

"We asked for your heart. You gave it warm. Alive. Whole."

A pause.

"That is not what most do."

"Most... do?"

"They give pieces. Fragments. They guard themselves."

The bear helped him sit.

"You held nothing back."

The boy tried to answer, but his tongue felt too large for his mouth. The room had returned; yet it still swam at the edges, as if his story had loosened the world's seams. He tasted salt. Not the sea's: his own.

I'm here, he told himself. *I'm still here.*

Only then did the bear's gaze sharpen, as if choosing what truth to place next into a heart already bruised open.

"Did I... pass?" the boy asked. His hands trembled.

The bear's expression shifted. Something like pride. Something like sorrow. Something like love.

"You did more than pass, child," it said softly. "You reminded us what a heart is for."

The animals drew closer. The bear looked at them. At the throne room. At the stars above.

"But before we speak of your path home," it said, "you must understand something." It turned its gaze back to the boy. "About your Blood Tree.

"And why it matters.

"Long ago," the North Bear said, "this land was green. Warm. At its centre grew the White Tree."

The bear's voice deepened.

"The tree held magic. Healing. Truth. But humans came and claimed that power."

A pause.

"In the war that followed, two griffins were slain. Their crystalline hearts were carved out and taken. One was hidden in a distant cave, where it still shines, silent... almost dead. The other was lost to the sea." The bear's gaze darkened. "Some say it twisted into a monster. But nobody truly knows."

The boy listened, unmoving.

"The White Tree fell, bleeding into the ground as it died. Eternal summer gave way to frost. Its magic soaked into the land – enough to preserve life, even as ice claimed everything.

"Men, stripped of the White Tree's hope, turned upon themselves. They loosed their darker natures and waged endless, hollow wars, thinning their own kind and abandoning their beliefs. In the ensuing chaos, they forgot us. They fell to the other side – into shadow, where memory cannot reach."

The bear's voice softened.

"The griffins withdrew into the depths of the sky and mourned their loss for centuries. They could not let it go. They are magical, yes – but inside, they are like you, child."

The bear looked at him.

"When the griffins returned, long ages later, they found their history erased, replaced by our own. In their mercy, they entrusted us with their tale. I told them that their future, bound to ours, would awaken memory and bring healing. So... they stayed.

"And then you came and gave them back a piece of what was lost. Not the tree itself. But its echo. Its promise."

The bear fell silent. Its gaze drifted beyond the boy.

"You are more than I foresaw for the future. Yet there is still pain within you – your gift carries it in its roots. You may not see it. But I do."

The bear's eyes were grave.

"A pain strong enough to begin another war. Because your grief doesn't stay inside you," the bear said. "Here, it *breeds*; it tugs at every old fracture until the world starts copying your wound."

"A war?" the boy gasped.

And then, with the North Bear's thoughts brushing his mind, he saw it.

Two bears, splitting. One white as light. One dark-golden.

A tree cracking down the middle.

You saw them divide, the bear's thought whispered.

You do not know why. Neither do they anymore.

The connection broke.

"I have lost count of the years," the bear said quietly.

The boy's chest tightened.

"Can they reconcile?"

The bear's eyes were sad.

"That is not for me to answer. Some things must break before they can heal."

I didn't know, the boy thought.

"But you... Your heart felt it," the North Bear said. "Deep in your wanting. But you were not ready. No one ever is."

The bear gestured. A pool of water formed before them on the floor – crystalline, glowing.

"Look," it said. "Tell me what you see."

The boy leaned closer.

At first, only his reflection.

Then—

He was younger. Six, maybe. Sitting at the kitchen table, bent over his homework.

His mother stood at the stove, singing off-key. She turned, laughed at something he said, crossed the room and ruffled his hair.

His father sat nearby, writing in his book, pretending not to listen.

A memory. A real one.

"Mum," he whispered. "Dad."

"This is the source of all magic," the North Bear said quietly, watching him. "All the power you have gained flows from one place. From love. From memory. From her. From him."

The boy could not look away. His mother's face. Her laugh. His father's smile as he watched them.

So clear. So present.

"To gain what you seek," the bear continued, voice heavy, to learn the final lesson of wisdom, to complete your journey... you must make a sacrifice."

The boy tore his gaze from the pool. "What?"

"The magic you carry is bound to memory. To grief. To love." The bear paused. "To become who you must be, you must give up this memory. The clarity."

"What does that mean?"

"It means you will keep them: in your heart, in who you are. But the memories will fade. Blur. Become less vivid. Less painful. Less..." The bear searched for the word. "Less consuming."

"No."

The boy stepped back.

"No. Absolutely not."

"Belief is one of your greatest strengths and weaknesses," the bear said gently. "But so is loss. You are not losing them. You are releasing the grip – the need to replay every moment, to search for what you missed, to let absence shape your breath."

The bear's eyes were kind.

"That is not love. That is haunting. And you deserve to be free."

"I don't want to be free of that."

"You will never be free of who you are. They are in your bones. Your blood. But you can be free of the pain."

The boy looked back at the pool. At his mother's face. At his father's smile. He tried to memorise every line. Every expression. To hold it forever.

"Wisdom requires sacrifice," the North Bear said softly. "Not because wisdom is cruel, but because growth requires space. And grief has filled you so completely there is no room left. For peace. For what comes next."

"But if I forget..."

Tears fell now, silent, striking the water. Ripples spread, warping his mother's image.

"What happens if I say no?"

"Then you keep the sharpness. The clarity. The pain."

The bear's voice was unbearably gentle.

"And you go forward unchanged. Still carrying the leviathan within you."

The boy thought of Kofi. Of the old man. Of the Crystal Tree. Of the South Bear's heart.

"They wanted me to be happy," he said.

The bear said nothing.

The boy drew a shuddering breath.

"Then I choose life," he whispered. "I choose..."

His voice broke.

"...to let them go."

The North Bear nodded.

"Touch the water."

The boy reached out.

His fingers broke the surface.

The memory fractured – not gone, but softened. The pain of the funeral. The smell of antiseptic. The lilies. The coffin's wood. The closed door. Some pieces vanished. Others remained, blurred, distant, like faces seen through a veil.

He could still see them. Still hear them. But it did not cut as deeply.

"What did I just do?" he whispered.

"You grew," the North Bear said. "You chose your future over her past."

The boy felt hollowed out. And lighter.

"Is this what healing feels like?"

"It is what beginning feels like."

"It's terrible."

"I know." The bear drew him close. "But it is necessary. And brave. And right."

They sat in silence.

Something important hovered just beyond his reach, and the effort of holding onto it made his head ache.

At last, the boy spoke. "You said you'd tell me how to get home."

The bear nodded. "To find Snowy – and your way home – you must find the pirate ship that took you."

The boy's stomach dropped. "The pirates?"

"They return to those waters every autumn. But to board

without being thrown overboard or hurt, you must disguise yourself. Become one of them."

"How do I learn that?"

The bear's expression darkened.

"That art is not mine. It belongs to my brother – the West Bear."

"The... West Bear?" The boy felt again the pain of the North Bear's vision. Light turning towards shadow. The split.

"My brother is guardian of transformation," the bear said. "Of masks and illusions. Of becoming what you are not."

It rose.

"I will guide you to the western fringe of my realm. There, I will show you another path. One that reaches the sunset lands more swiftly."

The boy stood. His legs trembled, but held.

"When do we leave?"

"Soon. But first... rest. Your body must mend."

The boy slept that night in the King's chambers. It was warm. Safe. The northern King watched over him.

He dreamt of the Blood Tree. Of his mother. Of Snowy. Of home.

When he woke, the North Bear was still there.

"Come," it said. "Let us visit your forest one last time. To say farewell. Then we depart."

They walked to the valley together. The griffins were already there – all four, circling above the dome. When they saw the boy, they descended.

They knelt.

"We thank thee, bearer of light," they said as one.[52]

The boy's eyes burned.

---

[52] We thank you, bearer of light.

"I didn't... I just wanted to pass the trials."

"Thou wast not striving to heal, nor warring against pain," the eldest griffin said. "That was true. Thou wast living."[53]

It sighed.

"And life heals."

It turned its gaze towards its brothers.

"Some of us still struggle to believe our father's voice lives again within thy tree. But we all agree – it is good to hear that voice once more."[54]

The boy nodded, unable to speak. He did not know what to say. So he bowed his head once and descended into the ice-cavern forest.

He took time to bid farewell to each tree, listening to their voices, saving the Blood Tree for last.

The red, crystalline tree, more than any other, stirred in him a sense of belonging. He lingered at its trunk, his hand resting against the wrinkled bark, drawing comfort from its warmth as crystal leaves and sprigs brushed his shoulders. The creatures he had shaped into being sang through the rustling.

I have to leave you, he thought.

Warmth pulsed beneath his palm.

But I will come back. Someday. I promise.

He stood there a long while.

Only then did he notice the fallen branches at the tree's base, glowing faintly. Between them lay seeds, fallen from dried fruits. He picked up the seeds and placed them instinctively in his pocket. Gathering the branches, he held

---

[53] You weren't trying to heal, nor were you fighting your pain. [...] You were right about that. You were just living.

[54] Some of us still struggle to believe our father's voice lives again in your tree. But we all agree – it is good to hear that voice once more.

them close. They softened and flowed in his hands, serpent-like. He wove them into his clothes.

Reinforcement. Protection.

I will carry you with me.

The Blood Tree's leaves stirred. Almost like approval.

The boy climbed out.

The North Bear was waiting.

"Ready?"

The boy looked back once, at the dome, at the forest within it, at the life he had nurtured.

"Yes."

The bear knelt.

"Climb on."

The boy mounted its back.

"Where we are going," the bear said, "is not easy. My brother and I... we have not spoken in a very long time."

"Why?"

"Because we chose different paths. And neither of us knew how to build a bridge back."

The bear began to walk. West. Towards the setting sun.

"Maybe," the boy said quietly, "I can help with that."

The bear was silent for a moment.

Then: "Maybe you can."

Snow began to fall. Each flake a memory. Each one a promise.

The boy held on. Heading west. Towards the next part of his journey.

Chapter XVII: The Road to Heaven

«Memory's price, or heart's full gleam,
A sacrifice, to chase a dream.
With dawn's first light, his journey's end,
In tales of old, his heart will mend.»

The North Bear loped west for three days. The boy rode on its back, watching the frozen landscape change behind them.

Green followed where they stepped.

Not at once – never at once. The Blood Tree did not conquer the North; it remembered it. In their wake, something stirred, cautious as a held breath. The magic born of the boy's blood answered the older power sleeping beneath the soil. Fine roots threaded outward, testing the frost, learning what these lands would allow.

The soil resisted, then slowly gave. Small things at first. Moss. Lichen. Tiny shoots pushing through snow.

By the third day, the boy looked back and saw a thin line of green stretching behind them like a scar healing.

"The Blood Tree's claiming this ground," the bear said quietly.

The boy touched the wood woven into his chest. Felt it pulse.

"Is that... okay?" the boy asked.

"It is life. Life claims what it touches."

They travelled in silence after that.

On the fourth day, they reached the western edge.

Ice met ocean. Grey water churned against white cliffs.

The bear stopped.

"Here," it said, "is where we part."

The boy climbed down. His legs were unsteady.

The bear turned to face him. Its eyes were deep. Sad.

"You taught me," the boy said. His throat tightened. "The trials. They weren't just tests. They were—"

"They were you learning what you already knew," the bear said gently. "I only held the mirror."

The boy's eyes burned.

"I'm sorry," he said. "I have to go."

"I know." The bear knelt, bringing its face level with his. "The West awaits. And after that... home."

"Will I see you again?"

The bear's expression flickered.

"Perhaps," it said at last. "If the path winds back."

It touched the boy's chest with one paw. "Remember: light and shadow are bound. You carry both now. That's not weakness. That's wholeness."

The boy nodded.

"Go," the bear said gently. "The passage lies there." It gestured down the cliff face.

The boy looked. Only waves – until he saw it: a narrow gap in the rock, half hidden by spray.

"Trust," the bear said.

A thin ledge traced the cliff's side, slick with salt. He found his footing and followed it. The gap breathed water. A sea-tunnel – half drowned, half breathing – where the tide slid in and out and left a strip of air above the black.

When he reached it, he looked back. A white owl, pale as old bark and silent as snowfall, had settled on the bear's shoulder – a small witness in a world of giants.

The bear, as if unaware, watched only the boy, paw raised.

The boy raised his hand. Waved once. Then stepped into

the dark.

The passage swallowed him. Above, the ceiling rose just enough to hold the air; below, the tide lapped at his ankles, already trying to steal more.

Stone bit through the thin sole of his boot. Water curled around his feet, numbing fast. He waded forward with one hand on the wall, the other held out like a blind man's, counting steps by touch.

The darkness was complete.

He reached for light out of habit, wrapping it in magic. It flickered. Died.

Wrong. This isn't about light.

He kept walking.

The water rose. Ankle-deep. Knee-deep.

Why did the tunnel never end? Where did it lead? Was there such a thing as an end?

The boy felt himself falling and flying at once, suspended between motion and release. Someone waited at both ends of the passage; he could feel it, though he could not tell how. No beginning, no end. No time. Only a scatter of moments that did not belong to his body.

He moved, but not as himself. His shadow ran ahead, leaping from moment to moment, like a sailor crossing islands that rose and vanished beneath his feet – not because they were solid, but because the sea between them had no shore.

He fought where *definition* closed in, where even a hint of light pinned the world into rules, and every movement dragged against walls of certainty.

Salt scraped his throat. His palm slid on wet stone. He swallowed air that tasted borrowed.

There was no reason, no conclusion. Only darkness, crowding close, unsure how to hold what it had been given. The shadows thickened. He felt them slide past like cold fish in a river: smooth, quick, strangely gentle where the warmth lingered, silent where gravity roared like thunder. Calm.

He was no one. Nowhere. Free.

And still, he wanted a foothold. Something tangible.

The moment that wanting took shape in the deepest recesses of his being, the current surged. A wind started, then stopped. Started again – like a breath testing whether it was safe to become real. The passage narrowed.

Then whispers rose, sound arriving as meaning before it could become words. Like wind through cracks. Like distant crying.

Turn back.

You're not ready.

You'll drown here, alone.

The boy's breath came faster.

The whispers wrapped their insidious tendrils of doubt around his ankles. Pulled.

Just stop. It's easier.

He stumbled. Caught himself. The water was waist-deep now.

You failed her. You watched her breath grow quiet and called it waiting.

Your father too, blurred into absence because you never learnt how to hold grief without worshipping it.

And Snowy? You'll lose that bear the moment you stop running.

The boy's throat closed.

"No," he whispered.

You're pretending to be brave. But you're still the scared boy at the funeral.

"I know."

Then why keep going?

The boy stopped. Water lapped against skin. Cold.

Why was he going?

To find Snowy. To get home. To—

To run. Like you always do.

"No."

Yes. You ran from the golden beach. From grief. From yourself.

The boy closed his eyes. He loosened his hands in the water. Not surrender – release. The current touched his fingers like a question. He let it answer. The whispers were right. He had run. But...

"I'm not running now," he said aloud.

The whispers paused.

"I'm walking towards something. Not away."

Towards what?

"I don't know yet. But I'm walking." He opened his eyes. The darkness was still complete. But he could feel the current. Water moving. Forward.

Follow the current.

He did.

Step by step. The whispers faded. The tunnel shelved upwards, and the water fell from chest to waist, then to his thighs.

After what felt like hours, light appeared ahead.

Dim. Grey. But real.

The boy walked faster.

The passage opened. He stumbled out onto a beach. Grey sand. Grey sky. For a moment it felt like the same shore from where he came. But the air smelt differently, like an autumn rain.

The western lands.

The boy dropped to his knees, breath tearing in and out.

I made it.

But the whispers lingered. Faint. Inside him now. Those were part of him too. The recognition came without words. He sat up. Looked back at the passage.

Dark. Waiting.

He reached into his pocket and found the Blood Tree's seed, warm against his palm. In the grey sand, he dug a hole, pressing the seed inside it. Covered it, his fingers spreading the sand slowly, as if learning the motion.

"Grow here," he whispered. "Where the light meets dark, and neither has to win."

Then he stood, brushed the sand from his hands, and looked up.

The sky was wrong. Not clouds. *Cloud*. Singular. Massive. A floating island. Suspended in the air, its presence chilling the lands that lay in its shadow.

The western realm, shrouded in fog.

The boy stared.

How do I get up there?

He touched the wood woven into his chest – the Blood Tree's grafted branches, living reinforcement he had braided into his armour.

Can you...?

The wood stirred. Warm against his skin.

Then moved.

The boy gasped.

Branches uncoiled from his chest. Crawled over his shoulders. Spread. Strange, like something that had learnt his shape was forgetting it.

The branches thickened. Lengthened. Crystal leaves unfurled.

Wings.

Wooden wings. Red-crystal feathers. Growing from his shoulders, spreading fine nerves and roots along the armour, mapping themselves to his muscles.

The boy tried to move them.

They responded. Stiff. Awkward.

I can fly?

He tested. Flapped once. His feet left the ground – barely.

Flapped again. Rose a foot. Dropped.

He learnt it the hard way: up meant pain, and pain meant resistance. He fell twice, caught himself once, and on the fourth try the wings found a rhythm – wobbly, burning, but real.

He climbed. Higher. Each heartbeat fought the wind, and with every beat the magic thinned. The shadow of the western realm loomed closer.

After what felt like forever, his feet touched cloud. Not mist, but weight: vapour pressed into substance, as though the West itself had taught it how to keep a promise.

The boy collapsed. Lay there breathing hard.

When he folded the wings, he saw that a few red-crystal feathers had dulled. The flight had taken a small payment.

When he could move again, he stood. Looked around.

The western realm spread before him. Towering trees, sculpted from aether, breathed through their bark, inhaling

and exhaling in slow, visible rhythms. Puffy mushrooms clustered at their roots, and delicate flowers shed petals into the breeze. All of it rested on mountains and valleys of cloud, where rivers of pure water wove through the open air. Everything here looked half-finished on purpose, as though the land itself preferred *becoming* to being.

And creatures. Everywhere. Winged monkeys. Dragons. Harpies circling. Ogres patrolling.

In the distance: a castle. Eight mushroom-shaped towers. Fires burning violet.

The West Bear's castle.

Hippogriffs wheeled above the fortress, drifting in great

herds that flickered like living flame against the misty clouds. At the main gate, between twin barbicans, a pair of wyverns lay coiled around the stone, their slow breaths spilling dark, poisonous vapour into the air.

The boy crouched low. If they saw him flying, they'd know he didn't belong.

He needed to hide.

He gathered cloud-leaves and crystal wood, weaving them into a cloak that blurred his outline. Then he moved. Slow. Careful. Staying low. It took hours to reach the castle's outskirts.

The boy hid in cloud-brush near a violet fire. Ogres and harpies lounged around it, talking, laughing. He listened.

Their speech unfolded in his mind as clearly as his own. The cries of beasts, the rustle of wings, even the low mutter of creatures he could not see – all of it arrived with meaning. That shocked him.

Then he understood. The North Bear's telepathic intrusion had changed his thinking more than he had ever realised, opening a way into understanding he had never known existed – until now.

"Oi, did you hear about Grolth's first time crossing to this rotten place?" one ogre chuckled.

"Yeh, it spit its lungs out, clingin' to a harpy's back, thinkin' it could glide on someone else's feathers. Poor storm-winged thing near snapped under that ogre stench. Taught Grolth how to fly fast... straight down into the dirt!" a harpy screeched.

Laughter burst around the fire.

"Dumbness costs ya," another ogre rumbled, older, heavier. Its massive foot crushed a crumbling cloud-stump inches from where the boy lay glued to the ground. "Shoulda listened to the elders. Ya know what they yarn 'bout the Flower-of-a-Thousand-Dreams?"

The boy's ears perked.

"Nought really," a third ogre muttered.

"Picture the place in yer noggin, give the bloom a poke, and – *whoosh*, off ya go. No path, no climb. Just *there*. Faster than shoutin' *ogre*," a harpy said.

"Yer buyin' that rot?" the ogre scoffed.

"Ya reckon I'd wag me chompers just to hear me own echo?" the harpy snapped.

"Makes smashin' and grabbin' easy," the older ogre added. It snorted. "But every path ya don't walk teaches the world somethin' about ya." The fire sighed, then popped, sending a brief hiss into the air, as if something stirred its sleep. "And the world's got a long memory."

The boy's heart raced.

A flower that teleports you anywhere. If...

A twig snapped under his foot.

"Whaddat?" A harpy's head jerked towards him. Eyes sharp. Feathers bristling.

The boy froze.

"Yer ears be playin' tricks, ya fidgety runt," another harpy growled.

But talons stepped closer. Sniffing.

The boy did not breathe beneath his cloak of leaves and shadow.

The scaled leg stopped inches from his face. He could see the ridging in it, the dirt packed into the creases of skin, the dull nick where stone had bitten too deep. Heat rolled off it, sour and animal.

"Nothin'."

The claws lingered. Shifted. One hooked toe closed on

nothing, scraping the ground. Then, at last, the foot drew back slowly, not turning so much as uncoiling, as if the thing it belonged to had decided, for now, to hunt elsewhere.

The boy waited until they settled back around the fire.

Then moved. Silent. Away.

The *Flower-of-a-Thousand-Dreams*. That was his way home. But flowers like that don't grow by campfires. They bloom behind gates, kept close, guarded, named only in boasts.

How to reach it?

The answer settled into him like a claw. *The West Bear would know*. But he could not ask – not plainly. Who would hand such power to a stranger? The question itself would have to wear a skin.

Or perhaps the North Bear had already given the answer. Follow the plan. Reach the pirate ship. Learn illusion. Learn how to stand as something else.

Becoming what he was not.

He was very close. For the first time since losing Snowy, the path ahead felt unmistakably his. Clear.

He looked to the castle, to the wyverns coiled around its gates. He would have to reach the West Bear – however the path demanded it.

Then Snowy. Then home.

He sank back into the cloud-brush to wait for nightfall – and decide what he would dare to become.

Chapter XVIII: The Lost Heaven

«In darkness, buried magic learns to burn;
At journey's edge, the sun holds back its grace.
Above, a realm in cloud and shadow turned,
Where promises of power take their place.»

The boy waited until midnight.

The fires burned low. The guards changed shifts. Ogres yawned. Harpies preened.

He moved through the cloud-brush. Silent. Slow.

The west tower was about three hundred feet away. Two wyverns coiled around its stones, one turning with the tower's rise, the other against it. Poison spewed in sheets from their gullets, spreading into a mist that crawled through the air.

This was heaven, he thought, *if heaven could rot, clouds turning to fortress, wings turning to weapons.*

He only had to reach the tower's blind side, the service arch swallowed by shadow, and stay unseen.

If I make it there, I can get through, he thought. He crept forward.

Two hundred feet.

One hundred.

A stone pressed into his knee as his weight shifted. His breath caught. The poison-mist changed note, tasting warm lungs. One wyvern's coils tightened, scales rasping against the tower. He coughed – just once, too loud.

Every head turned.

Run.

The boy ran. The half-dragons cried an alert.

Shouts erupted. Wings beat. Heavy feet pounded.

He sprinted for the tower. So close. Fifty feet. Thirty.

Something hit him from behind.

He crashed into cloud-ground. Hard. His armour folded wrong. Pain shot through his ribs.

Two heavy arms pinned him. Hot breath on his neck.

"Got 'im!" an ogre bellowed.

More surrounded him. Harpies. Furies. All weapons drawn.

A dark fury leaned close. Its eyes gleamed.

"We sniff out yer purpose, sprout," one of the furies crackled, its voice like metal against stone.

"Ye done good showin' up. Course we woulda snagged ya

sooner or later. Been waitin' for ye."

The boy's heart fluttered so hard it hurt. "I need to see your King."

Laughter. Sharp. Cruel.

"Oh, ye will," the fury said. "It's been waitin' too." A smirk. "Half curious am I why it keeps ye alive. To learn why ye came, no doubt. Simpler to feed ye to the blade."

The ogre pulled him up, brushing the dust from his clothes as if from a precious prize.

"Now, hoist them arms behind, if ye be so kind," said the ogre, resting a sharp edge against the boy's nape as it drew out a length of rope.

When the boy did so, the ogre drove the blade into the ground, then took his wrists and pulled them hard behind his back, winding the rope around them. A quick pull. A knot cinched tight. It was done before the boy could think to resist.

They dragged him through the gates.

Wyverns hissed as he passed. Poison dripped. The boy's

crystal-leaf armour steamed but held.

Inside the yard, a hippogriff's voice cut through the din.

"Let him be!"

"But he's mine, through and through." The ogre's voice sliced through the air with a serrated growl. "And I'm here to claim what's due – in blood and coin!"

"To the King we escort him," the hippogriff said firmly. "Untouched."

"He's ours!" the fury snarled. "Our bounty!"

"After the King's done."

"Joy thief, that's what ye be." The fury hissed, but stepped back. The ogre did the same. Their gazes stayed dark.

Two hippogriffs flanked the boy. One clawed through the ropes. The boy worked the stiffness from his wrists, easing the ache where the rope had bitten, and followed.

They marched towards the palace. As they neared the throne room, the boy glanced up at the dark obsidian, crenelated walls of the West Bear's palace, their shadows stretching across the path ahead.

"Will the King truly hear me out?" the boy asked softly.

"The King sees all, hears all," one of the hippogriffs replied. "Fret not, young one. Speak your truth."

"And what if my truth is not what the King wishes to hear?"

From the corner of his eye, the boy caught the severe glance of one hippogriff. A piercing admonition. Silence closed around them like a cloak.

The throne room was vast. Dark stone. Sulphur and a whiff of decay threaded the cold air. A stiff ceremonial escort of hippogriffs and grey furies stood along the sides. Unmoving. At the far end: a throne. Diamond. Gleaming with black fire.

And upon it sat a bear.

White fur. Wings unfurled like those of an angel. Not bear, not bird – something between. Dark robes draped its massive frame. Its eyes burned, golden and wild.

The West Bear.

It looked at the boy.

That gaze passed through flesh and bone, through stone and shadow. It possessed all. Knew it all.

The boy's chest tightened.

At last, the bear's gaze returned to him, and settled deep within. After a few interminable seconds, the bear withdrew its gaze. The pressure eased – not gone, merely contained.

"Welcome," it said. Its voice was smooth. Warm. Almost kind.

The bear gestured. "Let him stand alone."

The hippogriffs obeyed.

"I know why he's here," the bear continued. "He wants to

learn disguise. To sneak unnoticed onto a pirate ship. To go home."

The boy did not speak.

The bear leaned forward. The diamond throne gleamed dark under its robes. "Tell me," it said. "What do you offer? Why should I teach you anything at all?"

The silence stretched.

The boy swallowed. His thoughts scattered, then stilled. He saw it then – the bear's hunger wasn't for answers. It was for belonging. He aimed his words like a hook.

"I don't want to escape," he said.

The bear watched him closely.

"I want to learn your ways," the boy said, kneeling. "To become powerful."

A pause.

"Like you."

The bear's eyes widened – just enough.

"Like a son," it said softly. Something dark flared behind its gaze.

Then, louder: "Leave us."

The guards shifted, uncertain.

"I said *leave*." The bear's voice boomed.

Its paw betrayed a faint tremor, an involuntary movement at the edge of control. The West Bear did not look down. One paw closed over the other. Slowly. Deliberately. Then the claws pressed together, grinding, as if holding something in place.

It rose and turned its massive back to the child. Looked up at a painting behind the throne: a dragon in battle, wings spread, maw open.

The boy remained kneeling on the frigid stone. The guards filed out. The doors closed.

The King stood still, a solitary figure amid opulence, waiting for the last trace of movement to die and the air to settle. Silence spread outward, taking the space it had been denied.

Only then did the bear turn and approach one of the open fires burning too strong in the darkness of the room.

"My father was a human like you, lost in the magic of this realm," the bear said quietly. "I think my father was a bit crazy when he first imagined us."

The boy listened.

"He made four bears of mud and breathed life into them. Into us. He poured wanting into the mud like mortar, and the mud remembered its shape. A magic born of himself. He smiled. We smiled back." The bear's voice was distant. Lost. "He told each of us what to be."

It turned to face the boy.

"To the East Bear he gave a crystal and said: *'Give joy to all things. Bring life to all that is green.'* And it does. Weaves nests for hearts that fly away. Always building. Always losing. Always smiling."

The bear's expression darkened.

"To the South Bear he took its small paws and said: *'With these paws you shall do good before bad. Create delight without pain.'* And it does. Conjures life from the quiet of its heart. From nothingness, it gifts the certainty that even endings can be gentle. Still a child."

A pause.

"To the North Bear: *'Hold love close to heart before letting it fly into thoughts. Don't cling to the falling leaves.'* And it does. Watching things leave. Never grasping."

The bear's eyes fixed on the boy.

"And when my father finally thought of me, there was

nothing left to wish for. *'Just be yourself,'* he whispered – as if that were a shape, not a sentence."

The words hung in the air.

"A simple wish. But I wanted more. I wanted to be all of them. Joy. Delight. Wisdom. Everything. Anything to make my father proud. I wanted to be such a good son."

The bear stepped closer.

"But wanting everything... that's a coin with two sides. One is victory. The other is blood."

Its voice dropped.

"I tasted everything he gave me – joy, wisdom, delight – until there was nothing left to taste. I couldn't stop. I wanted more. Much more.

"And I chose."

The boy's breath was shallow.

"I chose death." The bear was close now. Looming. "I killed him. My father. While he slept."

The boy's hands clenched.

"After that, I conquered. I raised my claws and took all that I could reach. Built this kingdom. And now I have everything."

The boy found his voice. "Everything but the soul."

The bear smiled. Empty. The smile faded slowly in the shadows beyond the firelight.

"But I do not need it just to live," the bear said.

"Then you're not living," the boy said. "You're in between. Breathing but not alive."

The bear's gaze darkened, cold.

"You lost your centre," the boy pressed on. Words came faster now. "You avoided what mattered. My road gave me no choice. I had to endure. And I won't lose what made that endurance real."

"And what is that?"

"My soul," the boy said. "What I lived. What I felt. What remains."

The bear's eyes flashed.

"You pour yourself into every moment," it said. "You bleed into time."

"Yes," the boy said. His voice rose. "And in that bleeding, I'm free. I'm alive. I'm like music to thee—"

"Not anymore."

The West Bear's claws slid free, catching firelight as it lunged.

The boy threw himself sideways. Claws tore stone where he'd been. He rolled, scrambled up, backed towards the wall.

The bear advanced, slow as judgement.

"You speak of freedom," it said, "but you are tethered. Memory. Grief. Hope. Three chains braided into one, pulling you down."

It struck again. The boy ducked. Air screamed where the claws passed.

"I can lift them for you," the bear murmured. "No pain. No fear. Let me take the weight from you."

"No joy," the boy gasped. "No love."

"Exactly."

It lunged once more.

This time the boy was too slow.

Claws caught his chest. Wood and crystal split. He struck the wall and slid down, breath breaking apart.

The bear loomed over him.

"There are only two ways this ends," it said softly. "Yield your soul – or I take it. Only then will you be as I am."

Its breath smelt of ash and old winters.

"Free."

It leaned closer.

"My child."

The boy's vision blurred. His hand found the cut on his chest. His own blood. His own warmth.

I'm going to die here.

Snowy... I'm...

Then a voice – not in the room but under his ribs:

You're not alone.

The woven branches in his armour stirred, alive.

We're here.

A second pulse joined his heartbeat.

You carry us.

A cold breath he recognised, returned to him.

Stand.

His palm pressed to the wound. The bleeding slowed, as if the body remembered how to hold itself.

He looked up.

"No," he whispered.

The bear's eyes narrowed. "What?"

He rose – shaking, but upright.

"I carry them with me," the boy said, louder. "The bears. The trees. The people I lost. They're not a thing you can steal."

For one flicker something crossed the West Bear's face. Recognition. Longing. Loss. Then it hardened.

"So be it."

Claws lifted.

The boy's wings snapped open – instinct, not pride. Blood-crystal leaves flared into the firelight. He sprang upwards.

The bear launched after him.

The boy twisted mid-air, letting the winged bear overshoot, and landed light on trembling legs.

"You can't run from this," the bear said. "There is no escape. Haven't you learnt?"

The boy didn't run. He waited. As the bear dove again, the boy thought one word – *cage* – and the wood in his chest answered.

Grafted branches unspooled like tendons. Torch-frames from the walls softened. Hidden timbers in the palace woke and unknotted. In a heartbeat, living wood rose, coiled, and cinched.

The West Bear was dragged inwards, wrapped in a tightening cocoon.

A cage.

From inside it, the bear roared. Each word hit the walls like a shove.

"So many lessons," it snarled, claws raking. "Trust in darkness. Death. Rebirth. Joy without guilt. Wisdom through sacrifice."

The boy's breath drained, ragged; magic as well, fast.

"But lessons are only lessons," the bear went on. "Can you hold them all at once? Or will you split?"

A claw punched through the cage, splintering it.

The boy's stomach dropped.

It's too strong. I can't—

The thought lasted a heartbeat too long.

The bear tore free as if being reborn. The shattered cocoon was hurled aside, crashing into an open fire. Embers leapt into the fallen wood, and flame took it in one breath.

The boy spread his wings and jumped again. Not far enough. The bear's claw hooked his leg and slammed him to the floor.

One massive paw closed around the wings the boy had shaped – careful, almost tender.

Not striking.

Unmaking.

Layer by layer, it peeled them away, as one might strip bark from a living sapling.

There was no blood.

No scream.

Only the sound of something being unmade – not flesh, but belonging.

The bear tossed the wings into the fire. They caught fast, burning bright and brief. Light collapsed into ash. The boy, untouched, staggered anyway, pain ringing through him from somewhere deeper than skin.

The bear waited until the last bit of ash drifted up and vanished.

Then it began to circle.

"There is no magic left to help you," it said. "The question was never which lessons you learnt."

It stepped closer.

"It is this: which one will you become?"

A pause. A smile, thin as a blade.

"A mask – and my mercy. Or your truth – and the pain that follows, like weather."

It stepped closer still.

"Choose."

Chapter XIX. The Flower of Dreams

«In this tale of dreams and defiance,
A boy challenges the King's silence.
With every step, his journey's told,
In worlds of magic, dark, and bold.»

The boy's back pressed against the stone. His eyes were squeezed shut, as if he could bar the darkness by refusing to see it. Fear, raw and voracious, clawed at him from the inside, gnawing like a starving thing. Each heartbeat thundered in his ears, loud and lost, as though even his body no longer knew how to move.

The West Bear circled. Slow. Deliberate.

Claws scraped the floor. Each step drew closer.

"Choose," the bear said again when the circle narrowed to only a few steps.

The boy's throat closed. His wings were gone. His magic spent. Blood had dried on his shirt, and the wound in his chest throbbed beneath the crust.

I'm going to die.

Think. Buy time. Anything.

"Wait," he gasped, opening his eyes. His words rushed out, driven by the cold closing in. The air thickened, sharp with a metallic tang, crystallising around him as the bear's claws grazed the stone, each scrape ringing like a chain drawn tight.

The bear stopped.

"One question. Before—" His voice cracked. "Please." His words hung in the room, a fragile thread pulled from his pounding heart, catching for one breath in the room's dead air.

The bear's eyes narrowed. "Speak quickly."

Its shadow wings unfurled, and the air thickened – as if every breath now belonged to it. The sharp claws slid slowly back into the white feathers of the bear's paws. Its eyes remained fixed on the trembling boy.

The boy's mind raced. The ogres by the fire. Their conversation. The flower.

It's all I have.

"The Flower-of-a-Thousand-Dreams," he said fast. "Is it real?" The words hung between them, a question of hope or doom, impossible to grasp, impossible to ignore. As the darkness pressed closer, this single thought surfaced, unbidden and fragile.

Silence stretched, brittle and taut, as if the air itself might snap.

The bear stared at him.

Then—

Laughter.

Not cruel. Not mocking. Surprised.

The bear laughed – once, deep and startled – like it had forgotten it could. It bent forward, paw to its eyes.

Then it stopped, as if the sound had cost it something.

The boy didn't move. Didn't understand.

The bear looked at him. Something shifted in its expression.

"You're clever," it said. "More than I gave you credit for."

Its voice softened, steady at the centre of the chaos.

It sat. The threat eased – not gone, but contained.

"The flower," the bear said, "is not what the ogres believe."

The boy's heart fluttered. The tremor crept into his fingers as they found the cold stone floor.

"They think it a birth rite. A whisper. The child's first

dream. They call it the kiss that wakes the flower."

The bear's claws tapped stone.

"But that isn't magic," it said. "It's belief. The certainty that dreams matter."

It leaned closer.

"There is no flower of the ogres," the bear said. "As the child's dream deepens, an elder's hand rests upon the chest, light as a breeze through leaves. They say that somewhere beyond the dream something answers."

Its voice lowered.

"A flower kissing back the wind."

The bear straightened.

"A story that not even I can grasp," it said. "To make birth sacred. To make dreams worth keeping."

The boy's breath came faster.

Not real. Not...

"Then why..." His voice was small. "Why does the story survive?"

The bear's expression flickered. Recognition. Something like respect.

"Because," it said slowly, "sometimes a story works better than truth."

It rose. Approached.

"The flower isn't real. But believing in it? That changes things. Makes people fight. Survive. Choose."

The bear stopped.

"Is that why you asked? To buy time with a story?"

The boy met its eyes.

"No," he whispered. "I asked because I needed to know if hope could be real."

The West Bear, shadow made flesh in the shape of this dark angel, advanced with measured steps, its breath threading through the air like smoke from a dying flame. With each pace, the atmosphere thickened, pressing in on the boy with the certainty of nightfall. The bear's panting settled against his chest, heavy with oblivion, threatening to snuff out the fragile spark within.

"And now," the West Bear intoned, "prepare your flower for its demise."

The boy closed his eyes.

The flower isn't real. But belief is.

None of what happened to him here seemed believable. He wouldn't believe it if told. But it was real.

I might not be the same boy who drowned. But I'm here.

Yet in that suspended moment, between the weight of fear and the distant glimmer of hope, clarity came to him. The *Flower-of-a-Thousand-Dreams* was not something he carried. It was him.

A thousand versions bloomed at once:

The boy who stayed in grief, died slowly of sorrow.

The boy who forgot completely, lived hollow and shallow.

The boy who hardened into warrior, used pain as armour.

The boy who became monk, wise but distant, using knowledge to avoid feeling.

The boy who healed others while fearing loss himself.

So many possible selves.

Which one is real? he asked the flower.

The petals shimmered: *All of them. None. You are synthesis.*

He could hold sorrow and joy. Darkness and light. Loss and love. All of it, without breaking. He could remember his mother without drowning. Miss her without dying.

This was how he survived loss and chose life. This was why he was still breathing.

Not simple. Not resolved. The boy sighed.

All it takes is a wish, he realised. *A wish to kindle the dream, to feed the flame of belief already burning within.*

He thought about the golden beach. Not remembering – choosing it.

Sand between toes. Warm sun. Snowy's fur. Salt air.

That place. I choose that place.

"No," the boy said, opening his eyes. His smile was small and sad, but real. "Now, I'm ready. To be... just a boy. All of me. Complicated and contradictory. But alive. I'm going home."

The West Bear's claws hovered at his throat. A single drop of blood beaded on the pale skin – hot, precise, impossible.

"You think wishing will—"

"I've been dreaming in fear," the boy said, "but now the dream is gone."

All around him, flame began to flow. Warmth rose, and the West Bear's wings started to dissolve, fraying from their edges inwards as the heat took hold.

"This place isn't truth," the boy said.

"It's hunger wearing a costume."

He lifted his gaze, not to the dissolving bear, but to the place where the room ended and meaning began.

Towards the one holding these words.

"The truth lies within," he said softly, "in the endless blooming and fading of each fleeting breath."

Always unyielding – the Flower-of-a-Thousand-Dreams.

𝄞

A snap, a gasp, and the world shifted. Gone were the oppressive shadows of the dark den and King, replaced by the golden sands. Warm. Real.

The boy collapsed onto the beach. Gasped. His legs shook. He felt the wound in his chest, almost closed. Blood had dried on his shirt.

I'm... here?

He looked at his hands. Still bloody. Still shaking.

But the sky was blue. The sun was warm.

He stood and let his gaze hover over the waves, drinking in the depth of the sky, the rays of the sun.

"Amidst the tempest of existence, where dreams scatter like autumn leaves, a solitary bloom endures – the Flower of a Thousand Dreams," sang the boy. He remembered the tortoise's stone, its last stubborn sentences.

Each petal, delicate and small, unfurls its song beyond them all.

He buried his feet in the warmth of the sand.

And as its breath fades in dismay, its stories sink beneath the waves...

Every word made sense now. He knelt, drawing his hands beneath the tide of sand.

A wisp of sand upon the pages, weaving its dreams beyond the ages. The words steadied him, like a hand at his back.

"I've searched for you."

The boy's head snapped up.

Snowy stood ten feet away. Massive. White. Real.

"Where have you been?" the bear asked quietly.

The boy couldn't speak. His throat closed. Eyes burned.

He stumbled forward. Fell to his knees. Got up and wrapped his arms around the bear's neck.

Snowy was warm. Solid. Here.

"I'm sorry," the boy whispered. "I'm so sorry. I left you. I—"

"You came back," Snowy said. "That's what matters."

They stayed like that. The boy crying into white fur. Snowy patient and still.

Finally, the boy pulled back.

"Each journey ends," Snowy said gently. "It's time to go home. You're shivering."

The boy looked down. His hands were shaking. Not from cold. From exhaustion. From everything.

"But what's real?" he asked. "Nothing's the same. Nothing will be."

Snowy's eyes were kind. "You're real."

"Am I?"

"As real as a boy can be. As real as dreams when you choose to keep them."

The bear pulled something from its chest. A golden key.

Turned it in empty air.

A door appeared. Woven from starlight. Familiar.

"Don't look back," Snowy said, stepping through.

"Don't you worry about that!" the boy said, and followed.

The boy found himself suddenly surrounded by walls, familiar toys scattered like memories across the floor. Dawn light shone through the window. Warm.

The boy stood frozen.

When did I leave? How long was I...

He looked at his hands.

Empty.

He looked around. Snowy was...

There. On the floor. A toy. White. Plastic eyes.

The boy's stomach dropped.

He knelt. Picked up the toy. It was light. Cold. Unmoving.

No.

He searched its eyes for recognition. For warmth. For anything.

Nothing.

It was a dream... It had to be. And yet—

Something stung his neck. A thorn-like sensation.

He touched it. Pulled his hand away.

Blood.

Fresh blood on his fingers.

The boy ran to the mirror. Twisted to see.

A scar. Thin. Jagged. On the right side of his neck.

Like a claw mark.

Just like the old man's.

His breath stopped. The boy stood in his bedroom, holding a toy, bleeding from a scar that shouldn't exist.

The toy's glass eyes stared back. The blood on his fingers stuck and warmed.

"It can't be!" he shouted, unsettled.

"What?" came a voice from inside him. *"A dream?"*

Epilogue

The boy sat on his bedroom floor. Snowy in his hands. White. Small. He turned the toy over. Checked the seams. The worn patches. The places where fur had rubbed thin.

Just a toy.

But his chest ached anyway.

He set Snowy down. Touched his neck. The scar was there. Thin. Raised. Still tender.

Real.

He looked around his room. Toys scattered. Books stacked. Dust motes drifting through morning light.

Everything familiar.

Everything strange.

How long was I gone?

The clock said 7:02 AM. It didn't tell him *what day.*

Yesterday, or years ago – he couldn't tell. Or if he ever left.

The boy stood. Walked to the window.

Outside: empty streets. A few people walking by.

Bricks and cement. A pale grey sky fractured by buildings. Gulls.

He pressed his forehead to the glass. Closed his eyes.

Tried to remember.

The leviathan's teeth. Being stone. The Crystal Tree's song.

The South Bear's chocolate kingdom. The East Bear's tears. The North Bear's breath.

The West Bear's claws and wings.

It happened. I know it happened.

He touched the scar again.

But maybe...

"Breakfast!" his uncle called from downstairs.

The boy's eyes opened.

Uncle.

He'd forgotten the shape of ordinary days: who made breakfast, who paid the bills, who kept the house from collapsing around grief.

He looked at Snowy on the floor.

"Come on," he whispered.

He picked up the toy. Tucked it under his arm.

Headed downstairs.

Uncle was at the stove. Eggs. Toast. The smell of coffee.

"You're up early," he said without turning. "I heard you shuffling about."

The boy sat at the table. Set Snowy on the chair beside him.

"Couldn't sleep," he said.

"Bad dreams?"

The boy touched his neck. "I don't know."

Uncle turned. Looked at him. His eyes were kind. Tired.

"You look different," he said quietly.

"Different how?"

"Older." He brought him a plate. Set it down. "What happened to your neck?"

The boy's hand dropped. "I... don't know. It was there when I woke up."

Uncle leaned close. Examined it.

"Looks like a scratch. Does it hurt?"

"A little."

His uncle straightened. Touched his hair. "You should be more careful."

"I will."

He went back to the stove.

The boy ate. The eggs were warm. *Real*. He could taste the salt.

He looked at Snowy. The plastic eyes caught the light. For just a moment, the reflection wasn't the kitchen – it was sky, white and endless.

After breakfast, the boy walked to the beach by the thin strip of woods at the city's edge. Took Snowy with him.

The sun was warm. The waves rolled in. Gulls cried overhead.

He sat where he always sat. Where he'd sat with Snowy before...

The door. The old man. Before everything.

He set the toy beside him.

"Was it real?" he asked aloud.

The waves didn't answer.

He touched the scar on his neck. Raised skin, tender as truth. He looked at his hands. No blood. No crystal wood. Just hands – small, young.

But I remember.

The Blood Tree growing from his blood. The forest singing. The griffins' eyes. The West Bear's wings dissolving.

Every part.

"So it was real," he said.

The wind picked up. Carried salt. Carried something else – a voice, faint and familiar. Or his mind putting a mouth to the wind. Either way, he listened.

He looked at Snowy. The toy stared at the ocean.

"I don't know," the boy whispered.

He lay back in the sand. Closed his eyes.

The sun was warm on his face. The waves constant. His breathing slowed.

Maybe it doesn't matter.

Or maybe the dream was real enough to leave a mark.

The Flower of a Thousand Dreams was not a place at all,

but a practice: breathe, choose, become. A melody he could follow when the world refused to name itself.

I'm both: the boy who left and the boy who stayed. His hand found the scar on his neck. Traced it. Felt the raised skin. *That's what memory is. I'll never know for sure. Maybe that's okay.*

He opened his eyes. Looked at the sky.

Blue. Endless. No answers written there.

Just blue.

The boy sat up. Brushed sand from his arms.

Picked up Snowy.

"Come on," he said. "Let's go home."

He walked back towards the house, feet leaving prints in wet sand.

Behind him, the ocean erased them.

One by one.

Until there was no evidence he'd been there at all.

Somewhere, far away or very close, in the North or in his chest, a tree kept growing.

Red leaves. Crystal branches.

Holding what he could not prove.

Waiting.

More from River Linnsight

We hope you enjoyed reading *Bear Wings*. If you did, please consider leaving a review (on Amazon) to help other readers discover it.

Prefer reading digitally? This book is available as a Kindle eBook. Or you may wish to transform your reading experience with our vividly illustrated, timelessly elegant full-colour hardcover edition – a perfect gift for book lovers.

𝄞

River is a poet at heart, and pen and paper have seen much of his soul put into words. As a present to those who enjoyed this book, a further glimpse into River's universe – or a petal from the Flower-of-a-Thousand-Dreams – is humbly offered on the following pages. It is a different kind of adventure, learning and transformation – a brief lyrical one, that we hope you will enjoy and maybe want to escape into even more. When you do, River's upcoming poetry volume might be exactly what you need and resonate with.

You may also enjoy a sneak peek into one of River's next fantasy books, *Desert Wings*, the second instalment in *The Wings* series.

Hope

Hope is the iris of the world,
the place where love looks through

It leaves us like a mist,
returns as a star,
barely bright enough to follow,
yet

Unseen until it is felt –
a hush in the blood,
a wick threaded through the veins,
fed by what you give without words

You tremble at its touch –
like a spark

And you would trade anything
to be just... held

You teach it
to rise,
to fall,
to breathe

to love

(1998-1999, reviewed 2025)

Desert Wings

Chapter I: The scream

There is no beginning, and no end. Only now – the infinite passion of the middle, vanishing when it's written down. If the desert is a river, then I am the river; if the desert is devouring fire, then I am fire; if the desert is love and despair, then I am all that undoes me – unbinding what once held form.
– Marginalia on a forgotten page, Borges and Fellini

The stranger's feet had carried him here. He couldn't say why.

Twin suns – gold and crimson – blazed, staining the dunes in a single flare, bruising the shadows in their hollows.

Behind him, footprints vanished as fast as he made them. Ahead, the tree.

The last village had burned three days ago. Or three hours. Time slipped in this place, heat and shock blurring the edges until even memory felt sun-bleached. He could turn back. But to what?

Endless dunes rolled like the backs of beasts moving with the swell, their breath broken by scattered plants and ribs of bleached kelp – salt-fossils of a long-dead ocean.

Wind flayed the dunes with hunger, lifting grains of stone, timber and bone into their final indistinction, their gritty percussion hammering at anything that stretched above. Salt and sun-baked stone thickened the air; sandalwood lingered underneath.

The tree rose from the valley floor like an accusation: massive, bark veined in silver-green, crystal leaves chiming softly, scattering fragments of colour into the air. At its roots, gold sand mingled with red, weaving patterns he almost recognised. *Almost.*

His people had a word for trees like this: *kethara* – lifeblood, anchor, the root that holds the world when all else shifts. And for those who came unbidden to sacred ground: *thalan*. The one who crosses where he should not.

He pressed his palms together – a gesture for the dead. No one answered.

Were they ever his people, or only shadows passing through his life? Was he ever truly one of them?

His thoughts flickered, dissolving like wind-blown shards.

Here, none of it held weight.

The old pilgrim prayers had long since faded, swallowed by the hush of leaves and the quiet, untamed life reclaiming the *kethara*. Once, they gathered here to speak for their dead. But not anymore. The fire took them, and the silence kept what remained.

Something tugged at him. Not his feet this time. Deeper – inside the ribs, tightening his breath. The *kethara* wanted him closer.

This place remembers trials, a voice whispered in his mind. His own voice, but wrong – older, worn smooth by repetition. *And it repeats them until they are answered.*

He tried to speak. "Where am I?" The words dissolved into heat.

He'd asked that before. He was sure of it. Stood in this exact spot, shadow thin, hands empty, asking the same stupid question while something ancient and patient waited.

Was this the third time? The tenth?

Did it matter?

He remembered nothing of how he'd arrived. No road, no guide, no moment of crossing. But the chill in his spine whispered that this wasn't new. That he'd been here before, weaponless and without an answer, bound to something older than choice.

Fear.

He'd spent years learning to hate it, to treat it as weakness. Men of his kind didn't hesitate. Didn't freeze while others *burned.*

Yet here he stood. Trembling. Afraid of the tree, afraid of what waited in its shadow – afraid, most of all, of what he'd done the last time fear took hold.

The screaming. A woman calling his name through smoke while he ran—

He shoved the memory down. *No more running.*

He stepped forward, his footprints filling with sand behind – healing to oblivion.

Small things threaded into bark or vanished beneath sand. Beetles – needle-tailed, horns curved like scythes, shells catching light in faint runes.

Serpents with sleek bodies the colour of bronze and ash coiled in the shade of the roots. Their heads rose, tongues flicking – watching, tasting the strangeness of his presence.

Above, translucent dust-sprites hovered among the branches, wings faintly glowing. They had been singing, scattering pollen like embers, when he first spotted the tree from the ridge. Now – a held breath. Even the wind had stopped.

The tree had hushed them. Or he had.

He took another step. Heat pressed down. Sweat prickled across his skin.

From the cool shade, an oasis gazelle leapt – a streak of light, its crystal-tipped horns flaring once before it was gone. A lynx-lizard followed like a darker echo, sinking into the sand with a single bark – the thin lament of prey already lost.

His eyes tracked the gazelle, then the lizard. His heart

skipped a beat.

Then silence – the hiss of drifting sand tracing his skin, the only movement left in the stillness.

The ground trembled – once, then again, deeper, until its surface began to ripple. Far off, a buried giant moved.

The serpents at the tree's roots uncoiled, slipping deeper into shadow.

The sprites scattered, wings chiming like broken glass.

At first, only a shimmer of dust in the distance betrayed it. A shadow slipping beneath the dune crests. Massive. Deliberate.

Then – a head emerged.

Flat. Broad. Adorned with black feathers glistening like oil. Its eyes were dark and cold, intelligence stripped of warmth. Not hunger. Something worse. *Purpose.*

Its body followed, rising from sand in a smooth, muscular wave. Scales like cinder and obsidian caught the fractured light, each edged in crimson where the blood-sun touched. Its body stretched longer than any serpent had a right to be, coiling and uncoiling with the inevitability of tide.

It advanced. Fast. Effortless. Undeterred. Each lateral undulation sculpted the desert's rhythm into something primal, something that predated thought.

There is no beginning, he thought. *Only now, and the serpent closing in.*

The air thickened.

His hands curled into fists. His gaze flicked left, right, behind. Nowhere to run. He'd never outpace it. Even if he could – where would he go? Back into the dunes. The heat. The glare.

At least here, there was shade.

And a witness.

He swallowed once, then twice, the way he always did

when fear came. The scar on his neck *burned*.

His foot caught on something half-buried: a branch, thick and sharp-ended, fallen from the tree. He snatched it up, backing towards the trunk. The bark pressed against his spine, rough and cool. His knuckles whitened around the branch.

The serpent halted a few feet away. Coiled in the sand, its massive head lifted, then swayed with a slow, predatory precision – gauging him, deciding. Its feathers bristled, catching the blistering fury of the golden sun like blades heating in a forge.

It hissed – a sharp, astringent sound slicing through the heat, a claim of dominion. The young man, dwarfed by its immense form, raised the branch.

For a moment, they were still. Eyes locked. His heartbeat thudded so hard he was sure the creature could hear it.

Then—

A blur of black and crimson burst through a veil of dust. It attacked, hurtling forward.

The impact crushed the air from his lungs. The serpent's body coiled around him in a single, fluid motion – steel springs wrapped in scales. Its weight dragged them both down, sinking into the soft sand. The ground erupted, engulfing them in grit and fury.

He tried to scream. Couldn't. Pressure clamped his ribs, his diaphragm, his throat. Every muscle tensed, bracing against suffocation. Grains clung to sweat-drenched skin, stung his eyes, splintering sight into fractured choices – each a step towards death. Only the serpent's grip kept him in this one.

Not again.

The thought tore through him, sharp as breathless panic.

He would not freeze while others *burned*. He would not be powerless.

He still had the branch. Somehow, impossibly, he'd held

on. His arm was pinned against his side, but his fingers found the sharp end. He twisted, tore his hand free as agony knifed through his shoulder, and drove the branch forward.

It sank into scales. Into flesh.

Honey-coloured blood welled up – wrong, glistening – and mingled with sand. The scent hit him: sharp, like burning metal.

The serpent hissed – *pure fury*. Its coils tightened. Bones creaked. Above them, the suns wavered, red smearing into gold, gold drowning in red, their light collapsing into a single, blinding glare. His vision buckled, darkness feathering in at the edges. His grip slipped.

He'd struck it. And it had only made things worse.

His fingers went numb. The branch fell from his grasp, tumbling into the sand.

The serpent's head reared back, jaws opening. Fangs like daggers, venom glistening on their tips. Those points narrowed the world to a single truth: he was going to die here.

Above, the tree's leaves chimed – too sweet, too precise – like violins pulling tight to pitch. Branches groaned in cello tones. Beneath the sand, roots rumbled their double-bass growl. The *kethara* braced for its codetta[55].

The valley was singing. Or screaming. He couldn't tell which.

He could let go. Let it end. The serpent's grip would finish it – quick, efficient, final. No more running. No more nights waking with smoke in his lungs and that burning voice in his ears.

But—

---

[55] A diminutive of *coda* (It., *tail*); a short coda; it refers to a concluding part of a musical, literary or dramatic work; it also means a musical passage connecting the parts of a movement or the entries in a fugue.

No.

The word formed somewhere beneath thought, beneath fear. A refusal so fundamental it bypassed reason entirely.

Not yet.

The surrounding desert exploded in a burst of blinding colour. Every grain blazed crystal clear, every shadow knife-edged, perfectly defined.

Move. Move, you coward.

His hands shot up, catching the serpent's jaws as they descended. His palms slammed against fangs, against the roof of its mouth, against the wet heat of its gullet. He pushed. Pulled. His vision fractured – golden sun, blood sun, tree, sky, sand, all of it bleeding together into a single point of white-hot will.

He wasn't strong enough. He knew that. Could feel his strength draining with each heartbeat, each strangled breath.

But he pushed anyway.

The serpent's eyes met his. Black and fathomless. And in that darkness, something flickered. Recognition.

We've done this before, those eyes said. *We'll do it again.*

His muscles knotted, straining until he felt bones creak.

Then—

Something broke.

He was still breathing, the serpent's grip unchanged. Yet the fracture ran deeper, into a wall he'd built inside himself, stone by stone, year by year. The wall that said *don't feel, don't scream, don't...*

It shattered.

The scream ripped from his throat – primal, raw, shaking the valley. Tree, sky, sand – all rattled with the fury of life. It drowned the serpent's hiss. The coils jerked, shivering their length.

Not much.

Just enough.

Sand rushed in where its weight had been.

He twisted. Wrenched free. His lungs burned as air flooded back in – too fast, too much. His chest heaved, as though breath itself refused to leave him.

And he screamed again.

Like the first sound he ever made. The one that mattered.

Not flesh, not spirit – only pulse and will. A breath seized from some untamed depth.

And in that breath—

He woke.

Hands trembling. Split with splinters – *real* splinters. Blood tacky and drying, crusted beneath his nails. Sand in the creases of his palms.

Acknowledgements

In the tranquil hours of the night, River Linnsight found himself ensnared between the rhythmic beeping of life-support machines and the moon's silent whisper. As a doctor, his days were steeped in clinical precision, yet as dusk descended, his imagination unfurled its wings, spurred on by his lively, mischievous, yet endearing young children. Their unruliness and mischief subsided as the woven story captured their dreams.

On one such a night, River settled not at his old oak desk, but on the children's bedroom floor, shrouded in darkness, composing from the heart – a cup of steaming tea next to him, as a mundane blessing. He embarked on crafting a tale unlike any other. It was to be called "Bear Wings" – a story that sprouted from the depths of his dual existence.

The tale centred on a boy and his polar bear companion – no ordinary bear, but one endowed with magical powers, an entity wholly alien to this realm. Initially just a concept, the story took on a life of its own, inconspicuously blossoming over nights and weeks.

River's fingers pirouetted through the darkness (later on finding the touch of the keyboard), each motion a pulse, each phrase a breath. He infused his dual existence into the story, blending the doctor's meticulousness with the writer's artistry. The boy's odyssey mirrored his own – navigating memories, straddling disparate worlds, belonging entirely to neither, yet flourishing.

As the boy unearthed the fortitude within and embraced his distinctiveness, River discovered a fresh cadence in his prose. The narrative unfurled, a chronicle of bravery, acceptance, and the splendour of uniqueness.

"Bear Wings" evolved into a tale that resonated with many, a lighthouse for those feeling alien in their own skin or life. And as River healed bodies by day and caressed souls by night, he recognised that his two worlds were not merely linked – they were a singular continuum of his essence.

Thus, "Bear Wings" ascended, not solely within the confines of a book but also in the hearts of his children and partner, his inaugural readers and editors. They nurtured his creativity with their invaluable time and tender, patient counsel, spurring him to further cultivate his imagination.

Like any good saga, the story endures, thriving in the gaze and hearts of you, the readers of this fantasy. May your voyage be delightful and may your imagination soar beyond this point!

Thank you! To all of you. Thank you for your time.

About the author

River Linnsight: A Tale of Two Islands

In the vast ocean of existence, there are two isles that share the name River Linnsight. One, cloaked in the white garb of a healer, spends days and nights in the noble pursuit of mending the broken and soothing the ailing. This isle is where science reigns, and the stethoscope is mightier than the pen.

The other isle is a whimsical place, where words flow like a cascade of healing elixir. Here, River is the bard (yikes), the scribe, the weaver of tales that mend souls. This isle thrives on metaphor and meter, where the only code is poetry, and the only virus is writer's block.

Though these isles seem worlds apart, they are connected beneath the surface by the bedrock of River's being. For what is a doctor if not a storyteller of cells, and what is a writer if not a healer of hearts?

Beyond the realms of parchment and pulse, River finds solace in the digital garden of computers, tending to the bytes and bits with the same care as the petunias and peonies in the back garden receive in their turn. And while there are more hobbies in River's quiver, let's not arrow you with tedium.

So here's to River Linnsight, the dual-island dweller, whose pen is as sharp as a scalpel (oh, my!) and whose humour is as healthy as a heartbeat.

Stay in touch

Embark on a journey through River Linnsight's literary landscapes here:

https://riverlinnsight.com

or by scanning this QR code:

By visiting River's website, you may be able to leave comments and to subscribe to the mailing list. Subscribing is a fantastic way to stay updated on the latest tales spun from the dual isles of this unique storyteller. Don't miss the chance to be the first to know about new adventures and exclusive promotions. Happy reading!

You may also want to follow River Linnsight on social media.

Glossary

A

Adrift: Uncontrolled or without a clear purpose; for a boat, a person, or a plan.
Aether: A rarefied element that was believed to fill the upper regions of space.
Alabaster: A compact fine-textured gypsum, usually white and translucent; may refer to a colour reminiscent of alabaster.
Arcane: Known only to a few; secret, mysterious, or esoteric knowledge. As a noun: arcanum (plural arcana).
Attuned: Harmonised with or sensitive to something; able to recognise or understand it.

B

Barbican: Fortified outpost or gatehouse, typically at the entrance of a castle or city, used for defensive purposes.
Bask: Revel in and make the most of (something pleasing).
Bequest: Legacy; something left in a will.
Blimey: An expression of surprise.
Blood Tree: Sprouted from the boy's blood in a cave beneath the northern ice cap; its presence echoed the White Tree and began to re-awaken the frozen North.
Brittle: Likely to break, snap, or crack, as when subjected to pressure; having hardness and rigidity but little tensile strength (as glass).

C

Celestial: Of the sky or heavens; divine or otherworldly.
Chalice: A large, ceremonial gold or silver cup.
Chompers: Colloquial term for teeth.
Cinch(ed): To fasten something tightly.
Contempt: A strong feeling of disliking and having no respect for someone or something.
Corrupt: Dishonest or immoral.
Crystal Tree: An ancient tree that grew in the depths of the eastern lake, visible only on the darkest nights; it sang melodies that summoned both tears and smiles. Destroyed in the war between East and West, its seeds were planted by the East Bear and grew into the tree that re-birthed the boy.

D

Doth: Does; archaic third person singular of "do".
Draped: Covered with or as if with clothes or a wrap or cloak.
Dwindle: Diminish gradually in size, amount, or strength.

E

Embark: To begin (a course of action, especially one that is important or demanding).
Engulf: To enclose; to powerfully affect (someone); to overwhelm.
Err: To make a mistake.
Essence: The intrinsic nature or indispensable quality of something, especially something abstract, which determines its character.
Etch(ed): To cut a pattern, picture etc. into a smooth surface using acid or a sharp instrument (on metal,

glass, or, figuratively, into memory); the quality of a very clear and distinct memory.

F

Fickle: Marked by lack of steadfastness, constancy, or stability; given to erratic changeableness.
Frenzy: Great excitement or wild behaviour that often results from losing control of your feelings.
Fury (Furies): Chthonic deities of vengeance from Greek mythology, also called the Erinyes or Eumenides; a symbol of personified curses, thought of as ghosts of the murdered or cursed, often depicted as three sisters: Alecto (unceasing), Megaera (grudging), and Tisiphone (vengeance).

G

Galley: A kitchen in a ship; also a long, low ship with sails, rowed usually by prisoners or slaves (not the ship from the story).
Gnaw: The action of biting or chewing something repeatedly, often resulting in gradual destruction or the creation of holes; metaphorically, it describes feelings of worry or discomfort, as if something is persistently eating away at one's thoughts or emotions.
Great Tree: The backbone of the old world, final home to the East Bear at the heart of the eastern forest; it suffered from the split between East and West.
Griffin: A mythical animal typically having the head, forepart, and wings of an eagle and the body, hind legs, and tail of a lion.
Grotto: A small cave, especially one that is made to look attractive.
Gullet: throat or pharynx; neck.

H

Harpy: A cruel creature with a woman's head and body and a bird's wings and feet (mythology).
Heed: To give careful attention to.
Helm: Mechanism that steers a ship; position of control.
Hippogriff: A creature of Greek mythology with a griffin's (eagle's) head, wings, and claws and a horse's body.
Huffed: Simple past and past participle of huff; "*In a huff*" – an expiration of air in an irritable fashion.
Hull: Main body or frame of a ship or boat.

I

Intertwine(d): To twist or be twisted together, or to be connected so as to be difficult to separate.
Ire: Intense anger, wrath, rage.
Iridescence: The phenomenon of certain surfaces that appear to gradually change colour as the angle of view or the angle of illumination changes.

L

Leviathan: A biblical sea creature symbolising monstrous power or size; described as sea-serpent; was the name given also to an extinct sperm whale.
Liege: An old term for a lord or king to whom one owed loyalty and service (often used in the context of feudalism); it can also refer to a loyal subject or vassal.
Lieth: Archaic third-person singular of "lie".
Loam: Soil that contains a lot of decayed vegetable matter and does not contain too much sand or clay.
Lope: Run in an easy, relaxed gait or

stride, taking long, swinging steps.
Lore: A body of traditions and knowledge on a subject or held by a particular group, typically passed from person to person by word of mouth.

M

Matted: Twisted into a firm, messy mass. For example, hair or wool can be described as matted when it is tangled and dense.
Mire: *As noun* – swamp, bog, marsh; *as verb* – to become stuck or entangled in difficulty.
Mote: Very small piece of dust or similar material.
Mundane: Common; very ordinary and not at all interesting or unusual.

N

Noggin: Informally, it refers to a person's head; it can also mean a small mug or cup.
Nurture: To take care of, feed, and protect someone or something, especially young children or plants, and help them to develop.

O

Ogre: In children's stories – a fierce and frightening person/character, usually large, who eats children; an octopus-ogre – an ogre with octopus limbs, with a claw tip at the end of each tentacle.

P

Porthole: A window at the side of a ship.
Port side: The left-hand side of a ship when facing forward.
Preen(ed): (of birds) To keep feathers neat, trimmed, healthy; to groom or admire oneself with visible satisfaction, especially in a way that seems vain or self-important.
Prow: Forwardmost pointed part of a ship.
Pulpy: Containing or resembling pulp (the soft part inside the skin; used also for vegetables, fruits).

Q

Quench: To satisfy (thirst, desires, passion, etc.). To put out or extinguish (fire, flames, etc.).

R

Recesses: The hidden or hard-to-see parts of something or somewhere.
Reverence: Great respect; admiration.
Rigging: Ropes for the sails/masts on a ship.
Roil: To make turbid by stirring up the sediment or dregs of, or to disturb, disorder, or rile.
Runt: The smallest and weakest animal of a group born at the same time to the same mother; a small or weak person whom you dislike (informally).

S

Savvy?: "Do you understand?"
Scallywag: Someone (often a child), who has behaved badly but who is still liked, making it difficult to be really angry with them.
Scrawny: Someone or something described as very thin, and often not attractive.
Scurvy: A disease resulting from a lack of vitamin C; lame, disgusting.
Serrated: Broken, jagged, uneven, pulsating sound; notched, saw-toothed.
Sheer: Used to describe something very great, important, or steep.
Shelve(d): To incline (slope away) gradually.

Shroud: To hide something by covering or surrounding it.
Solace: Comfort or consolation in a time of distress or sadness.
Sorrow: Deep sadness or regret.
Starboard: The right-hand side of a ship when facing forward.
Steep: Rising or falling sharply; also, to soak in liquid (at a temperature below boiling).
Succumb: To fail to resist pressure, temptation, or some other negative force.

T

Tainted: Altered from a pure form; contaminated, corrupted, or damaged.
Talon: The sharp, curved claw on a limb of a bird or a lizard, used for seizing and tearing prey.
Taut: Pulled tight; not slack; also a situation filled with tension or stress.
Telepath: A person able to communicate thoughts directly between minds, not using any spoken language or physical signals.
Tempest: A violent storm.
Tempestuous: Involving many exciting and confusing events or feelings; tumultuous; as if hit by storm.
Tendrils: Thin stems which grow on some plants so that they can attach themselves to supports such as walls or other plants.
Toll: The sound of a tolling bell; also means a high degree of suffering or damage; also means a tax.
Twixt: Between.

V

Verdant: A rich green; covered with growing plants or grass.
Vessel: A large boat or a ship; also referring to a container used to hold liquids or a tube that carries liquid through the body.

W

Whimsical: Playfully quaint or fanciful, especially in an appealing and amusing way.
White Tree: Once growing in the North, the heart of the northern realm – born from an amrita seed in the sun-lion's heart and planted by griffins. It sang, holding magic of healing, truth, and life. Destroyed in the war between griffins and humans driven mad by the cyclopes' curse, its fall froze the once-verdant North.
Wrought: Past participle of "wreak"; *as adjective* – carefully made or causing a particular effect.
Wyvern: A mythical, large lizard-like creature, typically two-legged and winged, with a pointed, venomous tail (a snake-like stinger); known as a half-dragon, the wyvern in heraldry and folklore is seldom fire-breathing.

Northern Citadel
Western
Floating Realm
Volcano Island
Fairy Land
Great Tree
Southern
Mists
N
W
E
S

www.ingramcontent.com/pod-product-compliance
Lightning Source LLC
La Vergne TN
LVHW091034080826
845145LV00002B/489

* 9 7 8 1 0 6 8 5 1 5 3 3 0 *